Blame It on the Mistletoe

Wedding wishes and Christmas kisses!

You're cordially invited to the wedding of Millie and Charlie. As long as some well-placed mistletoe and the temptation of festive flings don't get in the way...

When best friends Millie and Charlie decide to conveniently wed, they launch into the whirlwind of wedding planning. But when Charlie's called away on business, Millie's left with best man Giles as her stand-in groom. It's all going well until the sparks between them start to feel very real!

Meanwhile, Charlie has reconnected with childhood friend Liberty. The gorgeous woman she's become knocks him off his feet, and soon he finds himself questioning his fake "I Do" pact...

As Christmas Day approaches, will they go through with the wedding of the season? Find out in

Christmas Bride's Stand-In Groom
by Sophie Pembroke

Miss Right All Along
by Jessica Gilmore

Both available now!

Dear Reader,

When the lovely and talented Sophie Pembroke asked me if I wanted to write a Christmas duet with her, there was only one answer. I love collaborating with other authors and duetting with Sophie is always a lot of fun. One evening plotting over dinner (in a bookshop of course) and we had the perfect scenario. Two best friends, a marriage of convenience. We all know how that story goes, right? Only what if there's a twist...

Charlie Howard has almost everything—looks, money, a title, a loving family... Only he has spent his whole life in love with the wrong woman, and now he doesn't trust himself where his heart is concerned. So what could be safer than marrying his best friend, Millie? But when work takes him to Scotland and into close proximity with his sister's best friend, Liberty, Charlie starts to wonder if a sensible drama-free future is really what he wants after all.

It was a joy spending time in a snowy Scottish castle with Charlie and Liberty. I hope you enjoy spending time with them too.

Love,

Jessica

MISS RIGHT
ALL ALONG

JESSICA GILMORE

ROMANCE

ROMANCE

Recycling programs for this product may not exist in your area.

ISBN-13: 978-1-335-21618-2

Miss Right All Along

Copyright © 2024 by Jessica Gilmore

For questions and comments about the quality of this book, please contact us at CustomerService@Harlequin.com.

TM and ® are trademarks of Harlequin Enterprises ULC.

Harlequin Enterprises ULC
22 Adelaide St. West, 41st Floor
Toronto, Ontario M5H 4E3, Canada
www.Harlequin.com

Printed in U.S.A.

Incorrigible lover of a happy-ever-after, **Jessica Gilmore** is lucky enough to work for one of London's best-known theaters. Married with one daughter, one fluffy dog and two dog-loathing cats, she can usually be found with her nose in a book. Jessica writes emotional romance with a hint of humor, a splash of sunshine, delicious food—and equally delicious heroes!

Books by Jessica Gilmore

Harlequin Romance

The Princess Sister Swap

Cinderella and the Vicomte
The Princess and the Single Dad

Billion-Dollar Matches

Indonesian Date with the Single Dad

Fairytale Brides

Reawakened by His Christmas Kiss
Bound by the Prince's Baby

Winning Back His Runaway Bride
Christmas with His Cinderella
Christmas with His Ballerina
It Started with a Vegas Wedding

Visit the Author Profile page
at Harlequin.com for more titles.

For Katy, thank you for asking me to be part of this duet. I always love working with you.

Praise for
Jessica Gilmore

CHAPTER ONE

'I AM SURE she asked for this song on purpose.' Charlie took a swig of his champagne and casually looked away from the dance floor. He was *not* going to give the bride the satisfaction of seeing him staring. Of seeing him display any emotion apart from showing that he was having a perfectly marvellous time, thank you very much.

Millie Myles, his best friend and long-suffering date, looked up from her own glass. A glass she had been staring into like it might hold the answer to many of life's problems. It was an outlook Charlie shared, tonight at least, but not one Millie usually took, and she was unlikely to be devastated by the wedding of society beauty Octavia Sinclair—and Charlie's long-term on/off girlfriend—to tech bro billionaire Layton Stone. The opposite in fact.

'*We are never ever getting back together?*' Millie grinned. 'I doubt the *whole* playlist has been designed to humiliate you, but with this song you might have a point. Ignore it, just look at me and pretend you're having a good time. That's what I am here for. That, moral support and to make sure you didn't do anything stupid during the vows.'

'Your hand on my knee was very helpful at the *persons here present* bit, thanks, but unneeded, honestly. I have humiliated myself in front of Octavia Sinclair for the last time. Octavia Stone I suppose she is now.' He took another swig. 'At least the champagne is good.'

'Too good.' Millie grabbed the bottle from the middle of the table and refilled both their glasses. 'Let's do a toast. Here's to being young, free and single…' There was an edge to her voice he couldn't quite decipher. It was a while since she had split up with Tom, but Charlie hadn't seen any signs that she was craving a new relationship; her floristry business was doing so well it seemed to take up all her energy. No wonder, she was *really* talented. Look at how she'd transformed the rather gloomy stone great hall belonging to Octavia's parents with her clever use of colour, her gorgeous designs and decorations.

'Does thirty count as young still?' Charlie asked doubtfully. 'According to my parents it's the *high time you settled down and thought about your responsibilities to the estate* age. Not much young and free there.'

'What responsibilities? You could hardly do more for the ancestral home, Charlie. You live there, work there...'

'And apparently I need to settle down and supply the next generation of overlords and worker bees.'

'Ah, that kind of responsibility.'

Charlie picked up his glass, dangling it by the stem. 'The problem is where do I start with the whole marriage and kids thing? I've only ever been serious about one woman and she's the one on the dance floor in the long white dress. You know, I always thought that one day Octavia and I would stop all the breaking up and dramatics, get married and live reasonably happily ever after.'

Millie raised an eyebrow so expressive it could have starred in its own video. 'Optimistic much? Seriously, take away the drama and what really was there, Charlie?'

'It wasn't all bad,' he protested. 'Far from it. We spent fourteen years together, on and off.'

'Mostly off,' Millie muttered and he nudged her.

'She's not just the drama queen and society queen bee everyone thinks she is. She has a really sensitive side, she just hides it from most people...'

'Which is why she's weaponizing Taylor Swift at her wedding?'

'Good point well made.' Charlie took another swig. This champagne really *was* going down a little too well. But then it wasn't every day a man had to sit by and watch his first and only love, his *ex-fiancée*, say 'I do' to another man.

He sighed. He'd been one half of the golden couple that had been Octavia and Charlie since his mid-teens and it took some getting used to the fact that they were absolutely and utterly finally over. In many ways the drama of their relationship had been an addiction. He knew it was bad for him and there was no happy outcome and yet he had kept on returning to her anyway.

But no more. The last break-up was the final one and it was time he moved on into whatever—or whoever—his future held. Millie thought so, his other best friend Giles thought so, his little sister Tabitha thought so, hell, even the family dog had a firm opinion on the matter. Octavia herself had clearly and publicly moved on, hence the expensive designer white dress and huge glittering rock on her left hand. In a way he envied her, her seamless transition to Layton. Charlie had no idea how to go about dating someone different after so many years with one person. All he knew was that he wanted his future drama-free. A sedate, adult relationship where disagreements were talked out and compromises reached and no one ever threw an engagement ring into a river.

'Those two definitely had an argument before the wedding.' Millie nodded at the couple dancing past them. 'They were glaring at each other in the church.'

'Were they? I didn't notice.'

'Because you were staring at the bride.'

'True,' he conceded. Although not so much in hope she would call the wedding off, as so many people here no doubt thought, but in hope watching her say 'I do' meant he could finally close this very long, drawn-out chapter.

Hugo and Charity, instead of glaring, were now wrapped around each other and kissing passionately. Charlie leaned against Millie. Bless her for trying to distract him. Again. He really needed to make more of an effort to be a more amusing companion; after all, he knew that she often found society affairs difficult, too conscious that she was the daughter of a cook and a gardener, here as Charlie's friend not in her own right. Which was, of course, utter nonsense. Millie was worth twice every other person here, with the exception of his sister Tabitha and Giles. Actually, scratch that, bloody Giles was acting as Layton's best man after all, just Tabby then.

He glanced over at his sister. Tabby was laughing as she chatted to her best friend Liberty, who looked up and met his gaze, her own a concerned query. Was everyone here waiting for him to do something drastic? They'd be disappointed if so. All Charlie intended to do was sample as much of the free champagne as possible and survive the day with his dignity intact. He smiled at her reassuringly and then looked away quickly. Once, long ago, he'd put Liberty in an awkward position, one right between him and Octavia, and that night still prickled at his conscience. She'd been far too young, just eighteen, and things had never been the same between them since, their easy, almost familial relationship, turned awkward and polite. If Tabby knew, about the kiss, about the way he had just walked away, about the way he had never mentioned it again or apologised, she would, if not kill him, maim him—she had always been very protective of Liberty. And he would deserve it.

So best not to even notice let alone think about how beautiful Liberty looked tonight. Charlie turned his attention firmly back to Millie, leaning in and lowering his voice as Hugo and Charity stopped close to their table, still snogging, hands groping places that really didn't need to be groped in public. 'I think she was hoping he'd propose before now. They've been dating long enough.'

'How long is long enough?'

Charlie shrugged. 'I don't know. Octavia and I were together for years…'

'Except you broke up every six months or so,' Millie pointed out.

'That might have been the problem.'

'Not the only problem,' Millie said. 'She was also awful to you, and the whole relationship was toxic, and I wanted better for you because I love you and you're one of my very favourite people.'

Why couldn't he be in love with *Millie*? She was his best friend, the kindest, the funniest, the most talented woman he knew. He pulled her in for a hug. 'And you're one of mine. You know, I don't think I'll ever get married now. I think Octavia was my one shot. If I couldn't make it work with her…' He shook his head. 'Except I have to, somehow. There's the estate. The title. The entail. My family expect—no, they need me to marry and carry on the line. But how can I? She was my one true love. How can I marry someone else?' Oh no, he had definitely drunk too much. He was getting morose and sentimental not to mention repetitive. One day he would be that man in the corner of the bar telling every unwary stranger who got too close about the one who got away. Even though he knew better, had known better for a long time.

'I don't believe that.' Millie took his hands in hers. 'I know it hurts now, but you have to have faith. I thought that Tom was my one shot…'

'And you haven't dated anyone seriously since. Remind me how this is supposed to convince me?'

'I guess *I* just have to have faith,' she said. 'I saw the doctor the other day and…'

She had *what*? Suddenly he felt a lot more sober. Was this why she had been so quiet over the last few days, lapsing into thought, not really listening or chatting on as usual? 'Is everything okay? What did they say?' He couldn't hide his worry and she squeezed his hand.

'Nothing like that,' she assured him. 'But I'd been having some tests for, well, women's stuff. And it turns out that my fertility is declining a lot faster than is usual for someone in their late twenties. They reckon that if I want to start a family, well, I need to either freeze my eggs and hope, or get started now.'

Charlie let out a long breath. 'I'm sorry. I know how much having a family means to you.' Millie had always talked about having lots of children. An only child herself, she craved noise and bustle and laughter. And if anyone would make a wonderful mother it was her. Life really was bloody unfair sometimes. 'What are you going to do?'

'Find someone to fall madly in love with me in the next forty-eight hours and marry them after a whirlwind courtship, settle down and have kids as soon as possible and live happily ever after?' she said wryly. 'I guess I'll look into getting my remaining eggs frozen. Hope that things work out later.' She shrugged. 'Not many other options, are there?'

'Maybe *we* should just get married,' Charlie suggested. 'Could solve a lot of problems.'

Millie laughed. 'Can you imagine? My mum would be over the moon.'

'So would mine.' He got to his feet and held out his hand. 'Come on. If we have to wedding, let's at least wedding properly and get a good boogie in.'

He'd been joking of course, when he had suggested they get married, but as he dragged her onto the dance floor he couldn't help wishing again that they *could* fall in love. It would certainly solve both of their problems.

'This might be the worst wedding I have ever been to,' Liberty Gray whispered as she held her glass up in what was, to her at least, a mocking toast to the bride and groom. 'Just ridiculously ostentatious and so self-important.'

'You're only saying that because a, you hate weddings in general and b, because you despise Octavia,' her best friend Tabitha whispered back. 'I mean, it's fair. I despise Octavia even more than you. And I haven't exactly warmed to the groom either.'

'Has he had excessive Botox do you think? Maybe he suffers that thing our teachers used to warn us about; you know, don't pull faces in case the wind changes? No one's face can be that taut naturally surely?'

'With his money if it *was* Botox then surely it would be a better job? Besides, he's the same age as Charlie and *he's* not resorted to fillers yet.' Tabby giggled, looking over at the next table. 'Poor Charlie. He's doing very well. I can't imagine why on earth he accepted the invitation. No one would blame him for swerving.'

'How long were he and Octavia engaged for?' As if she didn't know.

'In total two years but of course they had at least one of their many breaks during that time. You know, I accepted the invitation just to make sure she really did get well and truly married off and any threat to Charlie was finally over.'

If Liberty was being very honest with herself then she would admit that she had accepted

Tabby's pleas to be her plus-one for exactly the same reason. Not that she still had any feelings for Charlie—or Charles St Clare Howard as he was more formally known, the future Baron Howard, heir to a historic title, stately home and huge estate—she had grown out of them *long* ago. A schoolgirl crush, nothing more. But she was glad he was no longer in any danger of marrying Octavia. She wouldn't wish that fate on her worst enemy.

Despite herself she glanced over at Tabby's brother again. He had clearly had a glass or two of champagne too many, his blue eyes a little too glazed, his dark hair a little too ruffled, his tie slightly askew as he leaned against the pretty, curvy girl next to him, laughing as she whispered in his ear. Something that felt a lot like jealousy shot through her and she quickly dampened it down. Charlie Howard was a free agent, he could cosy up to whoever he chose.

Tabby followed her gaze and grimaced. 'Looks like Charlie is going for the drowning his sorrows option,' she said. 'Thank goodness Millie is keeping an eye on him. Don't they look good together? We always hoped that they would end up falling for each other, but Charlie has never been that sensible, or maybe Millie is *too* sensible to get tangled up with him in that way. She did the flowers and say what you want about Octavia and I usually do, but even I have to admit she has exquisite taste. Doesn't it all look marvellous?'

'Yes,' Liberty conceded. It did. The great hall was decked out in autumnal colours, warm golds and oranges softening the austere grey. And Octavia of course looked stunning, her rather sharp, cool angular beauty the perfect framing for the designer wedding dress—her second of the day so far. Her green eyes glittered with triumph and why not? She was marrying one of the richest and most successful men of their generation. He on the other hand looked like he was adding a rare object to his collection, his gaze possessive rather than loving and proud.

'I'm glad Millie is here, especially as Giles is best man. I have no idea what he's thinking agreeing to be part of the wedding party,' Tabby continued, throwing a disdainful look up at the top table. 'He's *Charlie's* best friend, apart from Millie obviously. I didn't even think he knew Layton that well.'

'Another way of sticking it to Charlie? It's not enough that Octavia is marrying someone else, he has to witness it, you are invited too, his childhood best friend has to do the flowers, his best mate is the best man. Is she just trying to hurt him, or do you think all this is a desperate plea for him to ride to her rescue?'

'You and I both know that Octavia Sinclair is quite capable of rescuing herself. I just hope that this shows Charlie once and for all that he is better off without her.'

'Me too,' Liberty agreed.

But two hours later it seemed unlikely that their wish would come true any time soon. What was Octavia thinking, cutting into Charlie's dance with Millie and insisting he dance with her? Had the woman no heart? Liberty took a sip of her wine and glared at the busy dance floor as Octavia threw her head back and laughed at something Charlie said, an intimate smile on her pouting mouth, looking up at him from under her lashes, a look Liberty had spent far too many teenage years trying to replicate without success.

Charlie's smile on the other hand looked forced, his posture tense, and Liberty's heart squeezed. The man might be a fool wasting his teenage years and all his twenties on a woman as mercurial and dramatic as Octavia, but she knew Charlie had truly loved her, had seen depths in her that nobody else had. Maybe he had been fooling himself, or maybe Octavia really did have a secret side she had only shown to him. But today she was behaving true to form, trying to reel him back in even though she had literally just married someone else.

Well, it might be her wedding day but that didn't mean everything had to go her way.

Before she had time to think through her actions, Liberty strode onto the dance floor, wishing she had bought a pair of flats as her feet protested the movement, and tapped Octavia on the shoulder.

'Mind if I cut in?' she asked sweetly.

The momentary look of shock and anger was so vitriolic that Liberty nearly took a step back before Octavia clearly remembered where she was and smiled.

'Of course, I've monopolised you for too long, Charlie darling.' She couldn't just leave it there, leaning in to press a lingering kiss on his cheek before sashaying away without a backwards glance.

'You don't have to dance with me,' Liberty said quickly. 'I just thought you might need a rescue.'

Close up she could see that Charlie was both more and less drunk than she had imagined.

'I would love to dance with you,' he said with an exaggerated bow. 'Shall we?' He held out a hand and she took it, flushing as his fingers closed around hers.

'Having fun, Liberty?' he asked as he whirled her into the middle of the dance floor. Charlie was an excellent dancer, she hadn't forgotten that, even though she hadn't danced with him since New Year's Eve eight years ago. A night she both tried to relive and forget in equal measure. Did he remember at all? She suspected so. He'd been a little distant with her ever since then, polite and friendly enough, but he had avoided ever being alone with her. Liberty's gaze dropped to his mouth and despite herself she couldn't help remembering how he tasted, how he had felt, how his kiss had been everything her romantic eighteen-year-old heart had wanted it to be. How she might have let things progress if Octavia hadn't shown up unexpectedly. How Charlie had left her with just one apologetic backwards look. How they had never spoken about it again. How she had tried to forget it and yet, despite several actual relationships since, that kiss was still the one she thought about when she couldn't sleep at night.

Eighteen-year-old her had been a romantic fool. Luckily twenty-six-year-old her was much more sensible.

With a start she realised that Charlie was still waiting for an answer. What was the question again? Ah yes, was she having fun. 'Not really,' she said honestly and after a startled look he let out a shout of laughter.

'Me neither,' he said. 'Tell me, are you nursing

a broken heart too?' His tone was self-mocking. 'Champagne is an excellent cure if so.'

'No broken heart, I just don't like big over the top weddings.'

'Don't let Tabby let you hear you say that,' he warned. 'Where would the Howard family be without huge weddings and glitzy parties? The more excess the better is our new family motto.'

Liberty laughed. 'Tabby knows how I feel, it doesn't mean I don't admire what you do.' The Howard family had taken their portfolio of expensive to maintain houses, castles and lodges and created a hugely successful events and location business, supplying the backdrops for myriad films, TV programmes and photo shoots as well as organising luxury and glamorous weddings and parties.

'So, tell me Liberty Gray, what kind of wedding would you want?'

'I'm not sure marriage is for me. It always seems like hope over common sense, most end in divorce anyway.'

Charlie laughed. 'So cynical, so young.'

Not cynical, experienced. Her family were single-handedly responsible for most of the divorce statistics, after all. 'Just being practical,' she retorted. 'But in the unlikely event I did succumb then I would want it to be small, intimate, something real. If I ever *did* get married, I want it to be forever.'

'Me too.' Their gazes caught and held, his smile rueful. 'I've had enough drama and ups and downs to last me a lifetime. I suspect you are the same.'

'I don't know how my mother had the energy to organise a big extravaganza for her fourth wedding or my father to think that the fifth might be the one to succeed, you know.' She was the only product of her mother's second marriage and her father's third, born into a dysfunctional theatre dynasty with a family tree so complicated it required pages of footnotes to figure it out. No wonder she had always been happier to spend her holidays with Tabitha. Howard Hall might be imposing and impressive, but the family were warm and welcoming and Liberty had always felt wanted there, something that wasn't always the case in the revolving door of her stepfamilies.

'Here's to real, Liberty.' Charlie had manoeuvred her back to his table where he picked up his glass of half-drunk champagne and held it up to her in a toast. 'To real and happy ever afters, whatever they may be.'

'Whatever they may be,' she echoed, toasting him back. For one moment as she looked into his still glazed blue eyes Liberty felt that old pull, a renewing of the crush that had kept her navigating towards Charlie during the years he had known her only as his kid sister's friend. But there were no happy ever afters for her where Charlie Howard was concerned. If she ever gave her heart away again—and that was a big if—next time it would be to someone who truly wanted it.

CHAPTER TWO

IT WAS A relief to get away from the wedding and back to Charlie's apartment in his Norfolk home. Howard Hall wasn't the oldest of the family houses, but it was the largest and most imposing thanks to the numerous bedrooms, drawing rooms, a ballroom, billiards room, library and all the other essential spaces for the landed gentry to rule their small fiefdoms from. Now, most of the house was let out for events and filming, the family occupying the East Wing, but Charlie's rooms were still more spacious than most people's entire houses and comfortably furnished with a mixture of priceless antiques and modern furniture.

'Nightcap?' he asked Millie who had collapsed onto a daybed where, according to family legend, at least one princess had once nursed a headache.

'Please.'

He took out two crystal glasses and filled

them with ice before adding a generous splash of cognac and then another before handing one to Millie.

'I think that went about as well as it could be expected to, don't you?' He grabbed his own glass and settled next to her. After all, he hadn't disgraced himself. In fact, he had even been the one to break off the dance with Octavia thanks to Liberty.

Despite his best intentions it had been impossible to ignore how beautiful Liberty had looked, her green silk dress clinging to slim curves, her hair autumn red. Maybe he should have told her so. But the memory of how he had once taken advantage of the younger girl's evident then-crush on him still made him squirm. Really, he owed her an apology although he doubted she even remembered; after all, she must have hundreds of men dangling after her.

Charlie grimaced. That wasn't as comforting a thought as it should have been.

'I give them six months. A year, tops.' Millie recalled him to the here and now. The wedding. Octavia was a married woman. For now at least.

But one thing he knew for absolute sure. She might be married for a week, a month or a year, but he was done. No more reunions, no more break-ups, no more drama. She'd made her choice and he'd made his and he chose a future where he was happy. Whatever that meant.

Charlie sipped his cognac. 'You're probably right. What do you think it is? The secret to an actual, happy relationship, I mean.'

'Well, my mum always said the secret was marrying your best friend.'

He leaned against her. 'Going by that rule, I should probably marry you.'

'Giles thought we should get married, too.'

Giles *what?* It was one thing for his friend to offer unwanted advice to Charlie but he had no right where Millie was concerned. And what was with Giles's sudden interest in Millie anyway? It wasn't as if he'd never met her before.

Charlie couldn't help feeling protective— after all, he knew his two best friends inside out. Charlie knew Millie's type and Giles was definitely not it thanks to his allergy to marriage and serious relationships. Giles was the epitome of no strings whilst all Millie wanted to be was tangled in all the strings. Besides, selfishly, it was bad enough that the two of them had never got on. The last thing he needed was to be in the middle of a fling gone wrong.

'Did he now?' he bit out. 'Interesting.'

Millie looked up at him. 'Interesting how?'

'Just that he said something similar to me. I

was warning him off you at the time,' he added grimly.

'Because I'm not good enough?' Millie sounded hurt and Charlie cursed himself for a tactless drunken fool.

'Because you're far *too* good.' Charlie squeezed her hand in apology. 'You're one of the best people I know, and you deserve everything you want in this world. And you want a family, and a happy ever after—and we both know that is the last thing that Giles wants.'

'But you do. You want the same things I do—to get married, be happy, have a family to carry on your name and title.'

Charlie leaned back and thought about it. He had to get married for the sake of the estate and the title, true, but actually he wanted more than that. He wanted to be with someone who genuinely liked him and who he liked. Someone who wanted to build a life with him, not keep tearing it down.

Someone like the woman sitting next to him. His oldest and best friend. Charlie looked at Millie who returned his gaze with equal speculation. *Millie.* He loved her, more than anyone apart from his family. No, she *was* family. He knew her inside out just as she knew him. And he wanted her to have everything she desired.

The babies she yearned for. Security, respect. He could give her all of that.

'*We* should get married.'

Had he said it, or had she?

It didn't matter, it was an amazing idea and Charlie was about to tell her so when she pressed a finger to his lips. 'Let's…we need to sleep on this. Sober up. Think things through. We'll talk about it in the morning.'

'And if we still think it's a good idea in the cold light of day?'

'Then we'll start wedding planning.'

Despite the copious amounts of alcohol—or maybe because of it—Charlie didn't sleep well. Every time he tried to sleep he saw Octavia, glittering triumphantly, Liberty laughing up at him—and Millie. His beautiful, adorable, clever, warm friend. She would make someone the perfect wife. Could that person be *him*? Should it? What would it mean for their friendship?

One thing he did know was that if they did go ahead, he would have to be in their marriage one hundred per cent; he didn't think either of them would be comfortable with a halfway house, and Millie deserved nothing less than his full commitment. Theirs might not be a traditional romantic love but he did love her, too much to hurt her in any way. Could he do it? Say good-bye to passion and romance? He thought so. It wasn't as if either had served him well in the past, after all. Besides, he was thirty. He needed to grow up anyway and didn't all normal relationships settle down eventually? No one could keep up the romance forever. And just yesterday he'd been thinking how much he yearned for calm in his life, for a marriage based on liking and respect. The kind of marriage he and Millie could enjoy.

Eventually Charlie gave up attempting to sleep and got himself and his hangover up, heading to the large combined kitchen, dining and living room to make some much-needed coffee and breakfast. The coffee had just brewed and the bacon started to crisp when he heard footsteps padding in.

'Did we agree to get married last night?' He had never heard Millie sound so tentative.

He turned to face her. She was wearing a pair of the pyjamas she had left at his apartment the last time she had stayed over, her hair bundled up, her face as tired and grey as he suspected his was. Millie. Familiar, comforting.

'That is entirely possible, yes,' he replied. 'Coffee?'

'God, yes, please. In a bucket, if possible.'

'Coming up, take a seat.'

He handed her a coffee, grabbed his and sat at the kitchen table opposite her. The silence stretched on and on. They *never* had uncomfortable silences. Was this an omen? A sign that one of them needed to point out that this whole idea was ludicrous? But he couldn't quite bring himself to speak. Last night he had decided to choose stability and happiness over drama and uncertainty. It felt like both those things were in his grasp.

True, if Millie hadn't told him about her fertility issues then he wouldn't even consider marrying her. She was still so young; she should have years to find a man she loved the way a woman should love her husband, but those years had been taken from her. Time was no longer on her side, and he could do something about that.

'We'd need to have rules,' she said suddenly. 'If we decided to go ahead with it, I mean.'

So, she was seriously considering it. Charlie tried to figure out how he really felt about their drunken idea becoming reality, but the queasiness and the thumping in his head made introspection difficult. 'You want to?'

'I think it's not the worst idea the two of us have ever had when drunk.' Every word sounded careful.

'No, that's still breaking in to see the new baby piglets on Mr Grange's farm when we

were on our way home from the pub that night.
I still have nightmares about Momma Pig chas-
ing us.'

She smiled as he had intended, the heavy air
lifting somewhat. 'Agreed. This is definitely a
better idea than that was.'

'But rules? What are you thinking?' Setting
ground rules seemed sensible. People so often
jumped into marriage with their expectations
unaired, with no idea what the other partner
hoped for. Look at Liberty's parents, serial ro-
mantics with devastating consequences for the
children and partners they discarded in their
search for happiness.

Better not to think about Liberty right now.
Or actually maybe it was better to remember
her and how relationship dramas could end up
hurting innocent people. That would never happen with Millie, surely, not when they had honesty and openness and integrity on their side.

'If the idea is to get married to have a family,
and be happy, we need to agree what that looks
like to each of us. Like fidelity.'

Fidelity. They had both been cheated on and
they had both been heartbroken by the decep-
tion. 'Absolutely. If we're married, we're married. Properly and faithfully and all that. I don't
want one of those marriages of convenience
where it's all just for the name and the status and

secretly they're both carrying on with someone else on the side.' He knew plenty of people in those kinds of marriages. Each to their own and all that but it wasn't for him. He wanted a partnership. Like his parents. They might argue and disagree and drive each other crazy but they respected each other too.

'Definitely not. So if we do this, we do it properly. The minute we say "I do" we're exclusive. What about sex?'

Sex. Charlie swallowed. He had never thought of Millie in a sexual way, not even as teens. She was gorgeous, obviously, but even so... He defaulted to joking. 'My understanding is it's kind of essential for the having of the children.'

'Not necessarily.' Millie looked as uncomfortable as he felt. 'It might be that my fertility issues mean that we need medical help anyway. There are options, if you don't want...'

Damn it. He was making his best friend feel like she wasn't desirable. And of course she was! She was beautiful! Look how Giles had been transfixed by her last night. It's just *he* had never desired her, which from a friendship point of view was just as well, but marriage changed everything. 'That's not... It's not that I don't want... I don't want a sexless marriage. If you're okay with that?' He didn't think any sentence ever had been more uncomfortable to say.

'Yes. Of course.'

That was that then. If they did this, they would have sex. Which would be fine of course. Eventually. They would have plenty of time to get used to the idea anyway. Millie clearly needed to think about starting a family sooner rather than later but a wedding took time to plan.

Millie set her cup down. 'So we're going to get married?' It was half question, half statement.

'Great!' He tried to smile at her. 'That's, I mean, happiest man alive and all that.'

'Charlie,' she said, reaching over to take his hand. 'Keep being honest with me, okay?'

'I will make you a good husband,' he told her. That was honest, he absolutely would do everything in his power to. 'A good father to our children. I think we can have a good marriage, Mills.' There was no reason why not, they had everything going for them, love, liking, understanding, compatibility. In fact, the more his head cleared and he could think, the more this seemed like a good idea.

'Thank you.'

'So, next steps. I guess we tell people. Time being of the essence baby wise and all that.'

'Yes, I guess we do.'

'Okay then. There's a post-wedding meet up at the pub. Let's start with Tabby and Giles. And then we can let the family know. Actually, we just need to tell Tabs. She'll spread the news quicker than a viral video.'

Once they told people, once it was out there, there would be no going back. Charlie had one failed engagement under his belt, he did *not* want two, but that was okay. He had an opportunity for a new start; he would be a fool to jeopardise that in any way.

Liberty had thought she would never drink again and yet here she was in a pub, surrounded by a lot of the same crowd she had been with yesterday, a gin and tonic untouched on the table in front of her. Tabby was clearly not suffering in the same way; her drink was almost finished as she flirted with a man in red trousers and a tweed blazer who Liberty knew she had absolutely zero interest in. But then to Tabby, flirting was as natural as breathing.

Charlie was at a nearby table alongside Millie and Giles. Liberty didn't want to be as aware of him as she was, to be shamelessly eavesdropping on the table, to notice how Charlie seemed nervous, looking at Millie constantly.

'Charlie! And Giles. The old gang back together!' A raucous voice cut through the noise.

Tabby broke off from flirting to glance over at her brother's table, eyes narrowed. 'Ugh, what's Ronan doing here? Total creep. Remember when he suggested we have a threesome? Pig. We were barely sixteen.'

'Did you ever tell Charlie?'

'If I told Charlie every time one of his drunken school friends came on to me, he would have done nothing but get into fights. I got my revenge. Itching powder and some STD rumours took care of him.' Tabby smiled and took another gulp of her rapidly disappearing drink. 'Is my brother actually going to say hi at any point?'

'Ronan! Good to see you, buddy. You weren't at the wedding yesterday, were you?' Charlie was saying.

'Not me, mate. I don't reach Octavia's exacting standards, but I wanted to come catch up with you all anyway. And to see how you were coping, of course. Can't be easy, watching the love of your life marrying another. Bet you went home and had a little cry last night, didn't you?'

'Ugh, I hate him,' Tabby hissed. 'Itching powder is too good for him. I want to chop his testicles off with a spoon.' She half got to her feet but before she could say anything, Millie spoke, her voice loud and clear.

'Actually, he went home with me.'

What? Had Liberty misheard? She glanced

at Tabby whose mouth was hanging open in utter shock.

'You see,' Millie continued, 'we just got engaged last night.'

Charlie was *engaged*? To *Millie*?

'What?' Tabby whispered and before Liberty could stop her, her friend was on her feet and barrelling over to her brother at warp speed.

'WHAT?!' Well, that was a lot louder. They had probably heard her on Mars. 'Did I just hear that right? Have you two *finally* got your heads out of your—'

'Tabby.' Charlie looked embarrassed. Liberty watched him carefully. Millie was flushed and obviously still angry with Ronan, Charlie uncomfortable, Giles as shocked as Tabby. Things didn't seem quite right.

But then, she would think that, wouldn't she?

Oh, good God. She didn't still have feelings for Charlie did she? Hadn't she learned her lesson a long time ago?

He didn't just not see her that way, he didn't really see her at all.

'Your you-know-whats,' Tabby continued at a volume far too loud for the assorted hangovers. 'And decided to do something about the *obvious* fact that the two of you are in love with each other?'

In love? Of course they were in love, look at

them. Gorgeous, best friends, the kind of people who knew each other inside out. They clearly belonged together.

'If you're asking if we're engaged to be married,' Charlie said, slowly. 'Then the answer is yes.'

Tabby squealed and Liberty wasn't the only one to wince as several sound barriers were broken.

'This is just *perfect*!' Her friend half fell over the table as she hugged everyone except a still shocked Ronan, managing to flirt with Giles at the same time. In many ways it was impressive how Tabby managed to multitask. 'No, you see the *reason* it's perfect is that we've just had a cancellation for a Christmas Eve wedding up at the house! Because you are getting married at the house, right?'

'Oh, of course?' Millie sounded uncertain. Not that Tabby took any notice, ploughing right on.

'And Millie! You've always wanted a Christmas wedding, haven't you?'

A Christmas wedding did sound very romantic. Not that Liberty was the kind of girl to dream of white tulle and flowers, she had made that clear yesterday. But if she was, then yes, a Christmas wedding would be perfect.

She didn't actually hear Millie answer but Tabitha was clearly taking silence as acquiescence. 'Of course! With your colouring, jewel tones and a winter theme will be *perfect* for you.' Tabby clapped her hands again. 'I'm going to go right up to the office and book you in now, before anyone else can steal your date. Mum and Dad are going to be so excited!'

She rushed back to Liberty.

'Libs! Did you hear? Charlie and Millie are engaged!'

'Yes.' Liberty smiled weakly. 'Congratulations. That's brilliant.'

She caught Charlie's eye and for one moment the whole pub disappeared and she was back in Scotland, in the snow, laughing in the pine forest as he threatened her with a snowball and with a sinking realisation she knew she wasn't over him at all—and he was further away from her than ever.

CHAPTER THREE

One week later

'THAT'S JUST NOT POSSIBLE,' Liberty repeated. Maybe if she said the words multiple times they would be true. 'We have a contract.'

'And *we* have a flood,' the woman at the other end also repeated, probably hoping that if she said the words enough times Liberty would accept them and stop arguing. 'I am really sorry, Ms Gray, but there is no way we can accommodate a film crew right now. The clean-up job will take weeks, the drying out alone...'

'I see. I'm sorry.' Sorry for herself as well as for the harried owner of the gorgeous Scottish castle where *Jingle Bells Highlander* was due to be filmed in just two short weeks. Liberty had costume people, props people, camera people, a ton of fake snow not to mention all the production and directorial staff heading to Scotland over the next fortnight. Permits had been secured, transport booked, storage organised,

catering found and she herself had been planning to travel up to Scotland next week to start
receiving shipments and making sure everything from catering to production suites were up
and running for the first day of shooting. And
now she had no venue. And as location manager, that was definitely her problem.

Liberty concluded the phone call, her mind
already whirring with alternatives. The good
news: one, she still had a couple of weeks to sort
somewhere, two, it was autumn which meant
the seasonal whirl of Christmas and New Year
parties weren't yet in full swing and somewhere might just be free for the eight weeks
she needed, three, she had the best contact list
in the business. The bad news? She had just a
couple of weeks to sort it out, the budget didn't
allow for more than one venue which meant she
needed a Scottish-looking castle, forests, lochs
(or a lake) and a forest all in the one place, and
it had to be in the UK because this was where
all the permits and the shipping was organised
for and oh God, this was an utter disaster.

Deep. Breath. Then contact list.

Ten calls later and she was feeling less than
optimistic. In fact, she was positively pessi-
mistic. No one had actually laughed at her, but
there had been more than a few sharp intakes of
breath, and ten reasons why two weeks' notice

for a film crew to take over whichever house
and land she had targeted really wasn't suffi-
cient. It didn't help that budgets were tight and
although they were paying an adequate amount
for a normal let, she couldn't throw money at
the problem. Funny how enough dollar signs
could melt most problems away.

Liberty ran her eye over her list again. She
had exhausted all her Scottish contacts; it was
time to move to the rest of Ireland and the UK
and hope some sweeping landscape shots and
enough fake snow would do the rest.

The trill of her phone interrupted her and she
snatched it up eagerly, hoping it was one of her
earlier contacts with a change of heart or even
better, the original venue telling her the flood
hadn't been as bad after all and if they just all
brought wellies…

'Libs?'

'Tabby?' Excellent, Tabby had been next on
her call list. Not only was she someone who
would offer the right amount of sympathy and
practicality, but she might know of some solution. After all, the Howards owned a successful venue hire business—it helped when your
ancestors had married into and built a nice collection of castles, stately homes and hunting
lodges. In fact…she ran through the properties in her head. No, none of them were quite

right, apart from Glenmere Castle and the family didn't let that out. Pity.

But much as she wanted to vent to her friend, Tabby only had one topic of conversation right now. Charlie's wedding. And Liberty really didn't need any more details or to hear how perfect Millie was.

In a way she preferred Octavia. At least she could hate Octavia but who could hate Millie?

Liberty had known Millie as long as she had known the Howards. Effortlessly cool, dark-haired, gorgeous curves, always there and yet somehow on the outskirts. Liberty had never really hung out with her, there was the age difference of course, but also Millie wasn't part of Charlie's smart society set and often melted into the background when his school friends were around. But she often saw the pair of them in the local pub deep in conversation, or laughing uncontrollably, or returning from long walks, the family spaniel Dexter at their heels. She had just never seen a *spark* between them. But maybe she just hadn't wanted to.

'You don't know of a nice Highland castle going spare do you?' Get the ask straight in. That way she could head off any wedding talk.

'What's this one called?

Jingle Bells Highlander.'

'Let me guess, it's about a grumpy but hot laird?'

'Tick.'

'Who discovers the magic of Christmas…'

'Tick.'

'Through…a winsome orphan?'

'Try again.'

'A Christmas elf?'

'Last go…'

'The love of a good woman?'

'Give that girl a prize. Only there will be no love for anyone if I don't find a venue promptly. None of yours are free and Scottish-looking are they? It's a shame you don't rent out Glenmere Castle. That would be perfect.'

'But we do! At least, we haven't yet, but the restoration is almost finished. We'll be listing it for next year soon.'

'How almost is almost?'

'We just need to sign it off…'

'Tabby, you might have just saved Christmas. Is there any way we can use it? It would be perfect!' It really would be. Even better than the original venue in fact. Grey stone and turreted, Glenmere Castle was the archetypal Scottish castle on the shores of its own small but perfectly formed loch framed by snow-topped mountains and surrounded by pine forests.

'I can't say for definite but I'll ask. We've put

in quite a lot of holiday accommodation, done up the cottages and built some lodges and there are the rooms in the castle itself, so we'd be able to manage cast and crew I should think. The village and pub would be delighted, they've been impatient for us to open up more, but obviously we couldn't while Grandma still lived there. She hated the whole events and location business, we couldn't have inflicted it on her at her home.'

'Tab, if you could sort this for me, I will owe you forever.'

'A drink will do. Look, our weekly meeting is this afternoon. I'll ask and get back to you with an answer by the end of the day. Will that work? It's going to be a fab meeting because we get to start wedding planning. I have *all* the ideas, I can't wait to tell Charlie my thoughts about ponies.'

Ponies? Better not to ask. 'You're a lifesaver.' Liberty finished the call, her heart heavy. She should be delighted that Tabitha might have the solution to her problem, but all she felt was flat thanks to the reminder that Charlie was getting married.

What had she expected? That once he was over Octavia he would realise that Liberty was the one for him, and come and lay his heart at her feet? She knew better. Liberty had long accepted that she wasn't the kind of girl anyone put first. Had long known to leave before she was left. To keep her heart safe at all times, even if that meant locking it away.

There was a reason Liberty preferred short, safe relationships, ones where feelings weren't involved. No risk of rejection, no risk of getting hurt.

It was a template that had served her well, kept her safe. And she had no intention of changing it any time soon.

'I know dear Millie will take care of the flowers, but…'

'Mum,' Charlie interrupted firmly. 'This is a planning meeting, for the business, not my wedding.'

'But darling, your wedding is business. Goodness knows you've kept us waiting for long enough.'

'To be fair the boy tried, not his fault the filly shied at the fence,' his aunt Felicity said. 'Let's hope this new gal has more staying power.'

Tabitha always said they should do a reality show about the running of the estate, a fly on the wall documentary about an ancient family grappling with the modern world and that their aunt would be the breakout star, ending up on *Strictly* and in pantos. Charlie suspected she was right.

'Dear Millie is so very reliable,' his mother said with a fond smile. She hadn't looked so happy when he had announced his engagement to Octavia, nor at the restoration of it. A short-lived restoration in the end, one Charlie suspected Octavia had engineered to target Layton. He was the kind of man who would find an engaged woman a much more interesting challenge than one readily available. Especially if said woman was engaged to an old school friend.

He waited for the usual pang but instead he felt…nothing. Good. He owed it to Millie to be happy and present in their marriage. It wasn't as if his family didn't have a long history of marrying for something other than love, for land or alliances, for influence or money. Marrying Millie for an heir, for stability and to make his oldest friend happy were some of the best reasons he could think of.

Only December did feel very *soon*. He'd expected more time to get used to the change in circumstances. But then again, from what Millie said, time wasn't on her side, so maybe it was better this way.

'Okay, to business.' Charlie got the meeting back on track. 'Anything to report from last week's events?'

Although each house and venue employed

professional events staff, the family kept a close eye on every detail, often managing bookings themselves, starting each week with a retrospective of the week before and a look at the week ahead before discussing details of events scheduled further out.

'Before we do that,' Tabitha said. 'I have a request. Liberty urgently needs a venue for her latest film, the one she secured has flooded, and she wondered if she could use Glenmere Castle for a couple of months. It's nearly ready, isn't it?'

'Poor Mother,' Felicity murmured. Charlie didn't know if she was referring to his grandmother's death of the year before or her certain horror at her home being used for commercial purposes. She had never approved of the letting out of the family houses, retiring to Scotland once widowed which meant, in deference to her, the castle had been kept for family use with only the estate cottages used for holiday lets.

'When does she need it exactly?' His mother, the undisputed inspiration and force behind the family business, pulled up the booking calendar, displaying it on the large screen at one end of the conference room so they could all see it. 'We haven't started to market Glenmere yet so it's free any time from the New Year. Rather a coup to have a film shoot for its first booking.'

'Well, that's the thing, she needs it in two weeks but she needs to be on-site pretty much straight away. It does mean income this year and it would be great to showcase it in use as we start to market it, wouldn't it?'

'Two weeks? Impossible. The insurance hasn't been sorted and there is still snagging to do. I'm sorry, Tabby, I would love to help dear Liberty out of course but...'

'Hang on,' Charlie said. 'How much is she talking about, Tabs?'

His sister named a sum and he whistled. It wasn't the most they had ever been offered, true, but they would be foolish to turn it down. 'The Glenmore restoration has been a substantial investment. The income from a whole estate let for two months would be very welcome, especially to the village and pub. I know they enjoyed some uplift from the builders, but they really need those cottages filled as soon as possible and there has been some grumbling that they will miss out on Christmas and Hogmanay trade. Why wait until next year if we have a booking ready to go?'

'But, darling,' his mother said. 'A film crew? You know how a film takes over the whole house. There's Queen Victoria's bed, and the Gainsborough. The insurance will be a nightmare, not to say that we're not set up for *any* visitors let alone a full venue takeover.'

Valid points but not insurmountable. 'I agree, one of us will need to be on-site for the first few weeks, possibly the whole time, but that's no reason not to do it.'

'Not me, point-to-point season will start soon and I need to be getting the horses ready,' Felicity said quickly and Charlie grinned at her. If horses weren't involved his aunt wasn't interested, but she loved Howard Hall and her historical knowledge was invaluable.

'Don't worry, Aunt Flic, I wasn't planning to exile you,' he reassured her, looking hopefully at his sister.

'Sorry, Charlie, but this is my busiest time,' Tabitha said regretfully. 'I want to help Libs, but between autumn weddings, photo shoots and the start of Christmas, not to mention *your* wedding, I have no free time between now and the New Year.' His sister spent much of her time at their double-fronted London Regency town house managing the many events and filming requests for its famous ballroom and perfectly preserved exterior.

'No, I see that. In that case I think it makes sense that I go.' As soon as he said the words Charlie realised it was what he had been hoping for from the moment Tabitha had mentioned the castle. Scotland. Fresh sharp air. Space galore. Time to breathe. Everything was moving so very fast, he needed to get away and process it all.

But, on the other hand, Glenmere Castle, with Liberty, wasn't exactly getting away. Unlike Octavia, Charlie had never enjoyed pulling other people into the middle of the constant soap opera of their relationship. But New Year's Eve eight years ago that was exactly what had happened. He could tell himself that he hadn't expected Octavia to show up at the castle; after all, they had been on one of their many breaks, he could tell himself it was only a kiss, he could tell himself that Liberty had been an adult, but the reality was that he knew she had a schoolgirl crush on him and he had had no business kissing her at all. Just as he had had no business being so aware of her at the wedding last week. No business noticing her in the pub when he was announcing his engagement to another woman. No business thinking of her in any way other than as Tabby's friend.

Maybe he had been too eager to offer to get away after all. But who else was there?

'You?' Tabby said. *'Now?'*

'What about Millie?' his mother asked.

'Apart from Dad, I'm the only person not tied to a venue and I don't think he wants to head to

Scotland for the whole of autumn,' he pointed out. Charlie and his father ran the entire family business, and although the events side was a substantial income generator there was a lot more to the Howard Estate. Charlie and his father had to juggle land management, tenants, agricultural schemes, shooting permits, woodland management and conservation as well as investments, stocks and shares and the myriad assets from art and jewellery to land all over the world. The Howard holding was ancient and substantial and Charlie had been bred to run it since he was a child.

'All I need is a laptop really,' he continued. 'Besides, I oversaw a lot of the restoration work at Glenmere so I am probably the best person to launch it. I can trouble-shoot issues on-site, make sure no one breaks Queen Victoria's bed and work quite easily. There's a lot to do, final snagging, getting the marketing done, some forestry and estate work I need to look at, I'd have to head up over the autumn anyway even if we didn't agree to let it. You know, even apart from helping Liberty, I think we would be idiots to turn this down.'

'But Charlie, you have a wedding to plan.'

He grinned at his mother. 'Darling, you have made it quite clear that you and Millie have a wedding to plan and my job is to agree to whatever you decide. I can do that just as well from Scotland. Besides, it's just a few hours on the train, I can easily pop down for anything essential.' He nodded at Tabitha. 'Get Liberty to send me the contracts and her timetable and list of requirements today and tell her we'll get back to her as soon as possible.' Charlie pushed away his doubts. Eight years was a long time ago and it was just one kiss. Ridiculous to even remember it really, and it wasn't as if he hadn't seen Liberty since then, she was Tabby's best friend, practically part of the family. Besides, he wasn't planning to head to Scotland for a clandestine fling, it was work and there would be an entire film crew on-site alongside them the whole time. He'd probably barely see Liberty. And of course, most importantly, he was now engaged to Millie.

Scotland in autumn and then on the cusp of winter, what could be nicer? Glenmere, with its air so fresh it almost hurt, roaring fires and mountains. Time away from weddings and all the responsibility that would descend on him when he said *I do*. He had meant his proposal—if you could call their conversation anything so conventional—and genuinely thought marrying Millie was both sensible and right, but it was all happening so quickly, they could both do with some space.

Now all he had to do was let his bride know that he would be leaving her to the tender mercies of his mother and sister.

CHAPTER FOUR

As soon as the meeting finished Charlie headed outside, managing to dodge his mother and Tabby who both had a long list of wedding-related queries for him. He breathed in, glad of the fresh air after the stuffy meeting room. The weather felt more autumnal today as October dawned, crisp and cool, the trees beginning to tinge orange and red.

He headed away from the house towards the ornamental lake, pulling his phone out of his pocket, and then paused, for once not sure how to approach his oldest friend. Usually, Millie messaged several times a day, sending photos or jokes or links to things she'd read she thought he might enjoy, and he did the same back to her. But the last week there had been near radio silence. They needed to get back to their old ease with each other somehow before their rapidly approaching wedding.

It wasn't the being married part that concerned him. He and Millie were totally comfortable together, they had been sharing beds since they were tiny, she knew all his most shameful secrets and proudest moments, his worries and frustrations and hopes and dreams. They would make a fantastic team, just as his parents did. But he had to admit the sex part was preying on his mind. He just didn't see Millie like that and it felt wrong to try and do so, despite their agreement to try and make babies the traditional way. To have a real and active sex life throughout their marriage. Was he naïve to think this could work? He hadn't even kissed her yet, not in the way he would be expected to as the wedding approached—maybe they needed to try and get it over with, just barge through the embarrassment.

Only now he was heading to the opposite end of the country for over two months. With a woman he had been attracted to once before. A woman he was spending far too much time thinking about given his newly engaged status.

Charlie frowned at his phone before finding Millie's name and, before he could overthink things, pressed the call symbol. The phone rang for a couple of rings before she answered.

'Hey.'

'Hey, is this a bad time?'

'No, no. I am just designing the colours for

that pitch, you know the big corporate event I mentioned.'

'How's it going?'

'Hmm, not quite there. It feels a little brassy at the moment. They want glamour but classy glamour, diamonds not rhinestones, you know?'

Charlie had helped plan enough weddings and events to know exactly what she meant. 'Do they want Christmassy colours?'

'Yes, but not traditional, so red and white are out which makes things tricky. I'll get there. I've just been distracted.'

He knew how that felt. 'We've just had the weekly meeting and there's an opportunity to let Glenmere Castle for a couple of months starting now.'

He could hear her surprise at the abrupt change in topic. 'Erm, that's good.'

'For a film shoot. Liberty is the location manager, you know, Tabby's friend.' Now why did he feel guilty just saying her name? Charlie winced; he knew why. It was because he could still see the flash of her grey eyes as she stared Octavia down, feel her hand in his as he led her into the dance. See the curve of her full mouth smiling up at him. He had no problem imagining kissing Liberty Gray. As long as he didn't turn fantasy into reality. 'She had a crisis. A flood or something. Anyway, we are stepping in and offering her a venue.'

'Okay.' Her unspoken question came through loud and clear: *why have you called me to tell me this? What's really going on, Charlie?*

'Anyway,' he hurried on. 'We're not quite set up for letting yet. Still snagging and so on and so the only way we could agree is if one of us is on-site for the shoot.'

'By one of us you mean you?' Millie had always known *exactly* what he meant.

'I know the timing is horrible...'

Was that a laugh or a cry? 'We are supposed to be getting married in less than three months, Charlie, and you are seriously telling me you are heading off to Scotland for the entire duration with everything still to plan?'

'Is this our first marital disagreement?' The joke fell flat and he winced. 'Mum and Tabby seem to have everything in hand...'

'But this is *our* wedding! I don't want to be steamrollered by your family. It might not be the most traditional of set-ups but that doesn't mean it shouldn't be meaningful, personal. If things go the way we plan, then this will be the only wedding either of us have.'

She was right, of course she was. 'I'm sorry, Millie. I'm an arse. I didn't think. You're right. I can tell Tabby we can't accommodate the booking after all…' Which meant letting Liberty down and he really didn't want to do that. He still felt like he owed her, for that thoughtless kiss, for her rescue at the wedding. But given the way she'd occupied his mind recently, maybe cancelling *was* for the best.

'Is that the alternative?' She sighed. 'I don't want you to lose out. I'm being silly, it's just a little overwhelming, you know?'

'I really do.' Charlie had reached the lake and he started to follow the path round trying to think of a way to balance the different responsibilities. 'Look, Giles is around. How about I get him to stand in for me for any wedding-related business? I'll be at the end of the phone whenever you need a decision, and he can be there for all the tastings and what-nots so that you're not alone and at my family's mercy. He's my best man after all. Let's make him earn it.'

'Giles. Right.' There was something indefinable in her voice. Was it disapproval? The two of them were a little prickly, they always had been; he didn't consider Giles's momentary interest in Millie at the wedding huge progress. But it was one thing for his two best friends to dislike each other, quite another for his wife and his best friend. Maybe it would be a good thing for them to spend some quality time together.

'If I was marrying anyone else I would want

you, obviously, but I think juggling best woman and bride is too much, don't you?'

To his relief she laughed, sounding much more like her old self. 'True! Look, of course you should go. I'll manage, no one is indispensable, not even the groom.'

'That's what Mum and Tabby think. They think I am completely surplus to requirements.'

'They're just excited for us. It's nice.'

'It is.' Charlie sank onto a stone bench and watched a pair of swans glide past, their almost grown-up cygnets not too far behind. He was glad they had decided to pretend to be in love. He wasn't sure his family or Millie's mum would have been quite as enthusiastic if they had known the real reasons behind the wedding. 'Are you?'

'Am I what?'

'Excited for us?'

Millie didn't answer for several seconds. 'I'm excited to get started with our lives. I kind of wish we could fast forward through the engagement and wedding part though.'

'We could fly to Vegas tonight.' He half meant it.

'Is that what you want?'

It was Charlie's turn to fall silent. Was it? Like Millie he would prefer to get on with the marriage now the decision had been made, to get past the awkwardness and the ceremony and just be them, Charlie and Millie. But at the same time he was glad of the respite Scotland offered him. 'Mother would never forgive me—nor would yours. And I know better than to upset the cook.'

He was still watching the swans. Didn't they mate for life? How did they decide which swan was their soulmate? Did they ever regret the decision? Wish they had gone with a different option? He and Millie had decided to get married so impulsively and she had been single for so long, floored by the news about her fertility. He didn't want her to have any regrets. 'Look, Millie...'

'Mmm?'

'I'm going to be gone for a while.'

'I know.'

'I meant what I said about fidelity, but we're not actually married yet. So, look, what happens in Vegas stays in Vegas. I'm fine with that.'

'Charlie, what on *earth* are you babbling about? I thought we decided not to go to Vegas?'

'I mean, if you want a final fling or two or whatever before you say *I do* then you should go for it. Sow those wild oats as my grandfather used to say.' Charlie had never understood what he meant before but now it made some kind of sense. When marriage was about things other than attraction and desire then was it so wrong to allow yourself to feel those things one last time?

'A final fling? Charlie, I have never had a fling in my life!'

'So maybe you should, while you can.'

'Hang on, is this about you?' Her voice sharpened. 'Are *you* having regrets? Do you want to be sowing oats?'

'Me? No. I'll be in the wilds of Scotland.' With Liberty. But he was certainly not planning on sowing anything with her.

'With an entire film crew and no doubt several eligible actresses, it's not as if you'll be a hermit in a bothy,' she pointed out. 'I'm sure there will be enough women for several flings. An entire magic porridge pot of wild oats.'

'I didn't mean it like that…' But he could see why she would think he did and given his recent thoughts he didn't blame her. Millie had always been something of a mind reader where he was concerned. 'I'm not interested in actresses or anyone. Honestly, Mills, this isn't me saying I want to sleep with someone before settling down with you. I've never actually had a fling either.' After all, he had only actually had sex with one woman before.

'Then maybe you *should* do some sowing too. Maybe you're right. We are about to commit to each other for life, maybe we should, oh I don't know, not go out there *looking* for a fling, but not feel guilty if the opportunity comes up. Argh. I can't believe I just said that, but I do mean it.'

'Okay then.' He watched the swans a little longer, turning her words over in his mind. 'This is weird. Isn't this weird?'

'A little. But we've always been able to talk about anything before. I think it's important we still do. And I think with you gone for two months or so and the wedding so close you're right. This is our last time to, you know, act on pure attraction rather than being sensible.'

'Millie Myles. Are you saying you're not attracted to me?'

'I'm working on it.' She laughed but he could hear the truth in her voice—and a tinge of worry. A truth and worry he understood all too well.

'We'll get there. Okay, let me break the glad news to Giles…'

'You're going to tell *Giles* that we are allowed to sleep with someone else while we're engaged?'

'No! He believes he has played Cupid and who am I to dissuade him? I'm going to let him know that his best man duties have expanded somewhat. You're okay with that? I know you and he can be a little off but he's a good sort when you get to know him.'

'Yes. Of course. Look. I better go, this colour scheme won't resolve itself. Bye, Charlie.'

'Bye, Mills.'

He ended the call feeling uneasy. He had a *carte blanche* for a no strings affair if he wanted it, but his marriage to Millie was about stopping the drama and uncertainty that had characterised his relationship with Octavia. He didn't need any last-minute fun, but he was glad he had made it clear Millie was a free woman if she wanted to be. Millie deserved all the love and happiness in the world after all. It was up to him to supply that once the wedding had taken place, but if she did get some fun in before then good for her.

But as he walked back to the house it wasn't Millie he was thinking of but the memory of the heavy fall of red hair down a slender back, the smile in dark grey eyes and the long-ago memory of a kiss in the snow. He hadn't been lying when he had told Millie he wasn't interested in actresses, he wasn't. And he had no right to be attracted to Liberty, especially after what had happened last time they were in Scotland at the same time. He had embroiled her in his messy affairs once before. He respected her far too much to do it again.

Which made spending the next few weeks with her an interesting challenge. No matter that he and Millie had just agreed to a get-out clause, Charlie needed to remember that he was a happily engaged man and any relationship with Liberty Gray was professional only.

'What did they say?'

Liberty snatched up the phone the second she saw Tabby's name flash up, heart hammering. There would still be two weeks of logistical and administrative nightmares if the Howards agreed to rent her the castle, but that she could cope with. Heading back to square one to start her search again was a far more daunting prospect.

'It's a goer!'

Liberty's hand tightened on the phone as she digested her friend's words, unsure if they had been spoken or she had just heard what she wanted to hear. 'It's a goer? Really?'

'Really and truly! Glenmere Castle is yours for as long as you need it.'

'Oh, thank you! I owe you, I owe you all. The biggest hamper you have ever seen will be wending your way this Christmas.'

'No hamper required, we're happy to help. Honestly, Charlie says the sooner we start monetising Glenmere the better, the renovations went a little over budget, I think.'

The sound of Charlie's name made Liberty's heart beat a little faster, a little harder, a little more painfully. For a moment, during that wedding dance, she had felt as if they had connected in some way, and despite her best intentions she'd been aware of a frisson of anticipation when he'd walked into the pub the following day. Anticipation which turned to shock the moment his engagement was so suddenly announced.

Shock because to the best of her admittedly champagne-addled recollections he and Millie hadn't looked loved up in any way at the wedding. Close, friendly, even intimate but not on the verge of being engaged. She'd actually thought there was something between Millie and Giles, which just showed her how off her radar was.

Shock because for a short time her old crush had come rearing back. It had taken several stern talking tos before she had regained her usual equilibrium. Liberty didn't do crushes, she didn't do vulnerability, she didn't do needy. She was independent and self-sufficient and that was the way she liked it, thank you very much.

With an effort she dragged her mind back to her actual job and the myriad things she now needed to organise. 'Great! Okay. Shall I send you the list of what we need, the shooting schedule, crew and cast names, bedroom requirements—can we use the rooms in the castle as well as the cottages? We may need rooms in the village as well…' Her mind was racing, where was her laptop? She needed to make lists, make all the lists.

'Absolutely. Look, I'm on my way back to London so why don't we grab dinner later and have a quick chat about immediate next steps? I know you're busy, Libs, but you have to eat…' as Liberty started to protest. 'I'll grab something and come to you so don't worry about cooking. But then I'll need to hand over to Charlie. I have a really full schedule in London, so much as I would have loved to work with you, I need to stay in town. But Charlie can manage most of his stuff remotely so it makes sense for him to be the family representative on-site.'

'Charlie?' Liberty's mouth was dry. 'On-*site*? But surely with the wedding so close he needs to be in Norfolk, not all the way up in Scotland?'

'To be honest, between me, Mum and Millie there isn't oodles for him to do.' Typical that the bride was at the end of Tabitha's list. 'The estate hasn't been snagged properly yet, you'll be the first to use it, plus we haven't even started to hire the event organiser, or the new general manager let alone train them so one of us really needs to be there. You'll be done by mid-December won't you? He'll be back in plenty of time for the wedding. We've decided on Christmas Eve.'

'Right.' Scotland with Charlie. That was unexpected. Unwelcome. But it would be different to the last time she had been at Glenmere Castle with him. It was autumn, not Hogmanay, she was older and wiser, and this was *purely* professional. Besides, she would be far too busy to even know he was there.

Liberty spent rest of the day organising her tasks into various to-do lists, checking the clock to see when she would be able to call LA and fill in the production company—always better to be able to deliver bad news with a solution in hand. She kept in contact with Tabby who arranged a call with the Howard Estate lawyer to draw up a contract similar to the one Liberty had arranged with the original venue and Liberty reciprocated with several long, involved emails to be sent on to Charlie about timelines, numbers of people and other requirements from electricity supply to parking arrangements—always more complicated when lots of large lorries were involved. At least they wouldn't need trailers, not if they were sleeping on-site, but they would need make-up rooms, a costume fitting room…she created another list.

'Charlie has promised to be in touch asap,' Tabby said as they spoke for the fifth time in an hour. 'He just needed to sort a few things with Millie today and then he is all yours.'

'Great.' Her heart gave a painful thump at the image Charlie being all hers conjured up.

What was *wrong* with her? She had been over Charlie for years! The painful and obvious crush she had had on him before The Kiss (she always thought of it with capitals) had subsided in a wave of humiliation and regret afterwards. Worse, it had cemented everything her family had made clear, that she was destined to always be the one left behind, unwanted daughter and sister…

It was painful to remember that back then she had still hoped that someone would *see* her, really see her, would want her, show her that she was enough. In some ways she should thank Charlie for confirming her worst fears. She'd used the experience to move on, to harden, to promise herself never to allow herself to be so vulnerable again. And she'd kept her promise, dating carefully, for fun only, calling time before anything deeper could emerge, and that strategy had kept her safe. She wouldn't allow anyone in and nothing and nobody could change that. Especially not Charlie Howard.

CHAPTER FIVE

FINALLY, THE LONG day was over. LA had been called, had exploded and then calmed down, new contracts had been sent over and forwarded to LA, details sent to the production company so that the cast and crew could be updated, logistics contacted, transport diverted and Liberty began to breathe again. She needed to head up to Scotland as soon as possible, ideally the next day, which meant packing and buying a train or plane ticket, but she was so tired she couldn't face either just yet. A very hot very deep bath and an equally deep glass of wine were more than deserved.

Only Tabby was due to head over. Liberty's brain hurt and she wasn't sure she was up to any more organising today but her friend had promised food and she *did* need to eat. Liberty opened her fridge to see if she had anything in and could put Tabby off, but the contents were too depressing to contemplate. A limp lettuce, a shrivelled handful of tomatoes, hard cheese, eggs of an indeterminate date. Great. At least she had time for the bath and the wine before Tabby got there.

Her buzzer rang, making her jump as she glanced at the clock. It was seven and Tabby wasn't due for another half an hour. She might be early for the first time in her whole life but it was unlikely.

'Hello?'

'Liberty?' Deep, masculine, familiar. 'It's Charlie, Charlie Howard.'

Charlie Howard was at her flat? Charlie Howard knew where her flat *was*?

'I know you are expecting Tabby but as I am going to be the on-site manager she thought it might be more sensible to cut out the middle woman and speak directly. I haven't had a chance to read all the emails you and Tab sent but we could go over them together now. If that's okay?'

'Um…' Her wine! Her bath! Her stomach grumbled. Her dinner. The dinner Tabby was going to bring. Hopefully the eggs were salvageable after all.

'If it's not presumptuous I bought food, Tabs said she was supposed to be supplying dinner and made it clear I had to step up,' Charlie added and Liberty leaned against the wall in relief as she pressed the button that released the door.

'Dinner is the magic word. Come on up.' She took a quick frantic look around the room, but it was too late to do any tidying now. At least she hadn't got any drying lingerie on display and if he wasn't impressed by the pile of romance novels stacked by the sofa then that was his problem.

She opened her front door and waited at the top of the stairs for him. 'Come in, this is me.'

'Nice place.'

'Thank you. It's not a stately home or anything but I like it.'

Liberty lived in a mansion block in Marylebone, in a two-bedroom first-floor flat with high ceilings, huge sash windows, a non-working fireplace, decent soundproofing and oodles of character. It was also way out of the budget of a freelance location manager, but her maternal grandmother, realising how rootless she was as her parents married and remarried, had gifted it to her for her eighteenth birthday.

'Your inheritance early,' she had said.

Liberty loved her home, the safety it represented, the sanctuary of it. Now Charlie Howard was here in it, something she had never expected to happen but admittedly had fantasised about once or twice. Okay, a little more than that. She tried to see it through his eyes: carefully chosen jewel-coloured sofas and chairs, an eclectic mix of pictures, plants everywhere—she needed to let her neighbour know they would need watering earlier than expected—filled bookshelves, books overspilling onto the coffee table and floor, a dining table covered with scrawled pieces of paper and her still-open laptop in the bay window. The small but functional kitchen was through a door on the far wall, two double bedrooms and bathroom further along the narrow hall.

'So,' he said, holding up the paper bag he had brought with him. 'Food? Do you trust me with your cooker? I promise I'm safe.'

'Cooker? Oh. Right. Of course, just through there.' She hadn't expected that Charlie intended to cook but sure enough, rather than a take-out the bag contained fresh pasta, vegetables, tomatoes and anchovies. Soon he was chopping the vegetables with a languid ease that made her stomach contract. *Stop watching his hands, Liberty.* 'Just a simple puttanesca,' he said as she handed him some wine and her ovaries immediately jumped to attention.

'Great. So, what did you want to discuss?' Keep focused on work, that was the way to survive the next few hours, weeks, months.

'How about we wait till we're eating?' Charlie suggested. So much for that strategy. 'How's your father? His last play got great reviews.'

'He's never been happier, apparently. Finally discovered the joy of a work-life balance and being a hands-on dad. Shame it took four starter marriages and six children he was less hands-on with before he had this epiphany.' She tried for dark humour, but knew she hit bitterness instead and Charlie shot her a quick comprehending look.

'It must be a lot having siblings so tiny. I'm not sure how I'd feel if my father suddenly presented me with a bundle of joy at his age.'

'Luckily for me, it's not the first time. I'm used to it. The truth is I don't see much of him, he wasn't that impressed when I decided on a career behind rather than in the spotlights. Not a boost for the family brand, you know? I guess it might be different if I was writing or directing.'

Charlie emptied the diced onion and garlic into the frying pan, the air instantly mouthwateringly aromatic. 'How about your older siblings, do you see much of any of them? Some of them act, don't they? Obviously Orlando does.' Orlando Gray, her oldest brother on her father's side, had recently been cast in a superhero film which, along with the success of her father's play and his new marriage had thrust her family back into the gossip pages and headlines. Not that they were ever far from them.

'Apart from me all his other grown-up kids are models, actors, reality stars or influencers—*they* love the spotlight like a proper Gray. Truthfully though I see more of them in the headlines or on social media or on TV than in real life. I don't really know them, any of the halves in fact.' Liberty had never thought of any of her seven siblings on her father's side and three on her mother's as anything other than *half*. There was just too much of a distance between them, and not just in age.

'That's a shame.'

She shrugged. 'I guess it doesn't help that I have never really lived with any of them. Dad's oldest two hated my mum and resented me and so *we* don't really talk. I didn't see much of Dad after he split up with Mum, Fleur, his next wife, didn't want me around which means I've never really known their three and, and of course the twins are young enough to be my own kids. And as for Mum's three, not only is there a considerable age gap but I was already at boarding school when Wren was born. I never spent more than half the school holidays at their house and never stay there now so always feel like some kind of distant aunt, not a sister. Some holidays I spent more time with your family.' She sipped her wine pensively. 'It's a shame Mum and Jack didn't have children, if they had they would have been closer to me in age, and Jack would have made sure I was part of the family. He was a great stepdad, I think I was more upset when she split up with him, than with Dad.'

Wow. Where had all *that* come from? Charlie had asked a polite question and she had turned her answer into a Wikipedia page about her family. She gulped another mouthful of wine and grabbed the bottle to refill it. 'More wine?' Although his glass was barely touched while hers was nearly empty. *Keep it together, Liberty. This is a working dinner, not a date.*

'Okay, this feels ready, bowls?' Charlie ladled heaped spoonsful of aromatic pasta into the bowls she dutifully provided and she took them through into the main living and dining space, hurriedly sweeping the piles of notes off the table before setting them down.

If her teenage self could see her now! Tête-à-tête at a table for two with Charlie Howard eating a meal he had cooked for her! Of course, in her teenage fantasies the evening would have ended with some serious snogging on the sofa and so, considering the amount of anchovies, onion and garlic in the pasta, it was probably a good idea that he was safely engaged and the evening was solely about work.

* * *

If it had been up to Charlie, he would have headed straight up to Scotland and met Liberty there, not turned up at her house to cook for her, but in the end he couldn't think of a reason to tell Tabby why her idea he swap in for her wouldn't work that wouldn't make her suspicious.

Tabby had always been very protective of her friend. She wasn't the only one, Charlie's whole family had taken Liberty under their wing after that first summer holiday visit when it had become painfully clear how little her parents cared where she was and who she was with. Soon Liberty had become a regular visitor. She often spent Christmas with them, most of the summer holidays. She had her own room at Howard Hall; even now Charlie's mum took her out for a birthday meal every year, met her for cocktails when in town.

If they knew Charlie had allowed her to become embroiled in his and Octavia's affairs, Tabby and his mother would have found it hard to forgive him. That was fine, he had found it hard to forgive himself; he wasn't sure he ever really had. Being drunk was no excuse. He still couldn't explain it. How Liberty had one minute just been Tabby's friend, part of the furniture—and the next infinitely desirable.

And then he had got back with Octavia and done his best to put that night, and the attraction he had felt for Liberty to one side. Which was why this sudden flaring up of interest was so inexplicable, not to mention horribly timed. He had to go back to seeing her as a long-standing family friend, nothing more.

Although Liberty seemed a little on edge at first, once they started to discuss her requirements and needs for the weeks ahead she started to relax, showing herself to be clear, focused and extremely professional. It shouldn't have been a surprise finding out just how sharp and knowledgeable she was. After all, she had grown up on film sets and backstage in theatres, had acted as a child and teen, but the job she had now wasn't one she could hold through nepotism alone; it required a forensic brain, a lot of spreadsheets and a terrifying amount of health and safety knowledge. Just like running a family estate with land all over the country in fact. Charlie couldn't help but be impressed. And daunted. She had to squeeze several months of planning into just two weeks and it was clear there was a lot of work ahead, no matter how organised she was.

'I am planning to drive up to Scotland tomorrow,' he said at last. 'You are welcome to come with me, unless you have a ticket booked to travel some other way?'

Now why had he offered that? It took over eight hours to drive to Glenmere Castle. A working dinner was one thing, a long journey in close proximity quite another.

'Changing my plane ticket is something I *haven't* got round to doing today,' she said, her smile tired. 'I originally meant to go up early next week, but of course I had already done several site visits. Luckily, I know Glenmere pretty well, but understanding how it will work as a set is very different to staying there as a guest. I need to plan where every van, lorry, cable will go, think about catering, airport pickups. At least it's not too far from the original venue...' Her voice trailed off as she clearly made several mental notes before she focused again. 'I didn't even answer your question. Yes, please. A lift would be amazing.'

Charlie eyed her with concern. She was pale, shadows under her eyes. 'Look, I'll clear up...'

'But you cooked!'

'...while you make a start on packing and then get an early night. I'll pick you up at nine, it's a long journey and I want to get started as soon as possible, but I'm aware you have had a long day already.'

'Nature of the job.' She tried and rather adorably failed to suppress a yawn. 'Early starts and late-night planning sessions are par for the course.'

'That's as may be, but we'll do no more planning tonight. Go on, start packing. I'll let myself out.'

Liberty's eyes narrowed and Charlie could see her considering arguing back before she laughed and capitulated. 'Okay, you're right. An all-nighter will help no one, I need to see what I am dealing with first. Thank you, for dinner and for the lift, and for bailing us out like this. I can't tell you how grateful I am. You have saved the film and my life.'

'I wouldn't want to deprive the world of *Jingle Bell Highlander*.'

'Maybe we could get you a walk-on part,' she suggested, her sly smile showcasing the dimple at the side of her mouth. 'You do have a kilt up there, don't you?'

'Like you I prefer to be firmly behind the scenes. Besides, no thanks required. We're not doing you a favour, this is business.'

'Do you always cook dinner for your business associates?'

'Only when a two-month let is involved.' Charlie stood up and collected their plates. 'Go on, the sooner you get started the sooner you can get some sleep.'

It didn't take long to clear up and Charlie left the flat, after saying goodbye to Liberty through her open bedroom door. She waved absent-mindedly, concentrating on the piles of clothes on her bed with a look of mild concern.

'Don't forget your thermals,' he called as he closed the front door. He half jogged down the stairs with a sense of relief. He could see Liberty and he working well together. She knew the estate and would respect it and the people who lived and worked there, and despite a couple of moments of silence, the evening had felt warm and relaxed. More, he liked her company. She had grown into an assured—and beautiful— woman. If he was single…

No. Even if he was single Liberty Gray was off-limits. Partly because she was his sister's best friend and getting involved with her was the very definition of messy, and partly because he still felt guilty about that kiss all those years ago. She had been too young to be mixed up in his and Octavia's drama and although he could honestly say Octavia had been the last thing on his mind when kissing Liberty, he *had* chosen her over the younger woman. Partly to protect Liberty. Octavia was never kind to women she suspected he was interested in, and he had tried to shield them rather than confront her. One of many things about their shared past that made

CHAPTER SIX

THE NEXT DAY Charlie collected Liberty on the dot of nine as arranged and they headed north out of London and onto the A1 to drive all the way up the east of England before hitting Scotland. Liberty was punctual and surprisingly lightly packed. Charlie was used to Octavia and Tabby, who had little in common apart from their tendency to need a huge suitcase for one night away 'just in case' and would have brought half their belongings for a trip this long.

'Got your thermals?' he asked with a grin and she nodded.

'Wellies and my puffer jacket too. I know what it gets like up there.'

'Forecast is gorgeous right now, sunny and fresh, but a lot can change between now and December.'

The traffic was slow heading out of London and Charlie concentrated on the road as Liberty fired up her laptop and immediately started tapping away. 'I might get quite a few calls,' she warned him. 'Will that annoy you?'

'Not at all, just let me know if you need the music turned down.'

'Can I ask even if I'm not on a call?' There was a tantalising glimpse of that dimple again.

'What's wrong with my music?'

'Middle-of-the-road men with guitars? Nothing. It's lovely.'

'Classic nineties indie.'

'Proving my point…'

'Feel free to change the station.'

'No, no, who am I to deprive you of lad rock? You are the driver after all.'

'Too right.' But Charlie found himself flicking through the stations until he found one with more of a mix and left it playing. He knew he was unadventurous with music, Millie teased him about the same thing. 'Okay,' he said once they were safely out of London and he had put the car into cruise control. 'Do you want to talk through where everyone is sleeping?'

'Do you mind? I know you have your own stuff to do.'

'I do but not while driving and, like you say, you haven't been to Glenmere for some time and the renovation means a lot of changes you're not up to speed on.' He paused. 'Obviously this is your gig but I've been giving it some thought.'

'Go on then. I'm poised.' She tapped her keyboard in demonstration.

'It makes sense to put the director in the apartment we have designated for the general manager. It has its own sitting room and study as well as a small kitchen, so they will have everything they need whether they want time alone or private meetings whilst at the centre of everything.'

'Agreed.' Liberty typed quickly. 'Okay, let's do the actors next.'

'How many and do you think they will prefer a cottage or a room in the castle itself? It's all been done up since you last saw it,' he added. 'Everything is redecorated, no more sharing cold bathrooms with half the enamel missing off the bath and power free showers! En suites all round. There are ten guest bedrooms in the castle itself. Guests also get use of the breakfast room, games room and sitting room. Plus there's the library, restaurant and bar which are open to people staying on the estate too. But of course, with a whole estate hire we can be more flexible around who uses what.'

'Let me see.' She ran her finger down her screen as she counted. 'The main parts are the hero and heroine of course, her best friend, the housekeeper, groundsman and the pub owner, the hero's mother and his childhood best friend.

There's also his little sister, but she will need a two-bedroom cottage because her mother is chaperoning.' Liberty read through the list again. 'So that's eight, leaving two bedrooms for the assistant director and producer. The rest of management can be in cottages. How many bedrooms does the pub have again?'

'Eight. And we have six cottages and eight new log cabin lodges with thirty-two bedrooms between them. There are also four tree-houses and two new domes on the other side of the loch but if we can avoid using them I would prefer it. The tree-houses are supposed to be all-weather but I want to check them out in more extreme weather before anyone stays there and the domes are really only meant for a night or two, not a long stay. They really are just one room with a screened off bathroom. But we can use them for any visitors I guess. Some of the villagers may be willing to do bed and breakfast as well.'

'Okay, that's forty rooms. We have two make-up artists, two hairstylists, three for costumes, then there's camera, electrics, scenery…' Liberty muttered to herself as she typed furiously. 'I'd rather not have anyone share, but I think we might be in luck if I call on those bed and breakfast rooms. I'll keep a couple spare as well for any visiting producers or other dignitaries, but it's good to know about the domes which sound very intriguing by the way as do the tree-houses. You must have spent a fortune.'

'Fortune is the word,' Charlie said a little rue-fully. Glenmere had been the biggest invest-ment the estate had made for years and it had given him more than one sleepless night. 'We did consider just doing the house and cottages and adding all the rest later, but with so many workpeople on site already and so much dis-ruption we just went for it. This film of yours is a godsend to be honest. Everything ran over schedule as well as over budget so we haven't even started marketing as a holiday and event destination yet. This gives me some breathing space to get that started. We might even pull in some of those crucial Christmas and Hogmanay bookings for this year.'

'More than glad it's worked out. We need you just as much, don't forget. Okay, extras can be bussed in and we've been in touch with the Ed-inburgh agencies, but if we can recruit some regulars locally, I know the producers would prefer that. The downside is not having profes-sionals on set, but the upside is it helps keep lo-cals onside and invested in the film and means fewer costs. Casting calls and training...' She continued to murmur to herself before sitting back with a relieved 'I think that works. I'll send it through to the producer's assistant for a second pair of eyes. I did accommodate him, didn't I? Oh! What about you? Where are you going to go?'

'Family apartment—we kept four bedrooms, a dining kitchen, boot room, sitting room and study in the west turret. I really don't want any strangers in there, we don't let family spaces, but you are of course welcome to a room there if you need one.'

Charlie knew it made sense to make the offer, it sounded as if Liberty didn't have many rooms to spare, and Tabitha would think it odd if he didn't. But Charlie wasn't sure that having her so close was really the wisest move. He was already far too aware of her every shift, the way she muttered to herself when concentrating, her soft throaty laugh, the way she twisted her hair when speaking.

Funny, he had known Liberty Gray for half his life, but he was wondering if he really knew her at all as a woman in her own right, not just as Tabby's BFF, the wide-eyed girl with a crush on him they had both pretended to ignore until the time they didn't.

She wasn't a girl anymore, he reminded himself. Liberty Gray was all grown up.

'So what's the plot of this masterpiece?' he asked, more to distract himself than because he really wanted to know. The first couple of times he had worked on film sets in one of his venues he had been fascinated but if familiarity didn't breed contempt, it did breed a lack of curiosity. It turned out filming meant a lot of waiting around.

Liberty turned to him. 'So, first thing, these films can appear formulaic and easy to mock but you know what? They bring a lot of pleasure to a lot of people. They're not as easy to write or act in as they seem.'

Charlie recalled the pile of romance novels he'd noted on Liberty's floor. She had eclectic and wide-ranging tastes; there had also been a good amount of crime, fantasy and other bestselling popular titles in there as well as a smattering of classics and some poetry and nonfiction, but she obviously enjoyed a bit of escapism and why not?

'Noted and understood. I didn't mean to sound disparaging. No,' he corrected himself a little ruefully. 'I did, I was after a cheap joke. I'm sorry and won't again.'

'It's not Shakespeare as my father would pointedly say, but it still deals with love and growth and other universal themes. Both lead actors are hard-working and pretty down to earth and the director is really good at her job, so we are in luck there. Okay, so the heroine, Shelly, is an American who hates Christmas…'

'I thought all Americans loved Christmas?'

'Not this one because it's the anniversary of the day her parents split up. So, she's in London for a conference and has arranged her flight back on Christmas Day to avoid the festivities but before then she has booked a couple of days in a spa that promises Christmas-free time. Only her driver gets lost and instead of ending up at the spa she ends up at a Scottish castle belonging to our hero, Lachie, who has just inherited it and was wondering how he's going to keep it going.'

'I can have a word with him about an events business if you like? Hang on, how did her driver end up in Scotland?'

'The spa was there, keep up! Anyway, he offers her a bed for the night and she agrees but is horrified because the castle is over the top Christmas ready and it's all her worst nightmares, only she wakes up to find she is snowed in and can't escape. Meanwhile he is all grumpy because this might be the last Christmas in his family home if he has to sell and he doesn't know how to face telling his mother and sister.'

'Tricky. My advice is to enlist the mother and sister. Mine have all the best ideas.'

'His sister is only ten but okay. Anyway, cue

snowball fights and sledging and hot chocolate in front of fires and visits to the pub and a *let's put on the nativity right here even though we are all snowed in* moment with a real donkey and carols and everyone pulling together to make it the best Christmas ever, led by our very own hero and heroine and before you know it the snow has melted, and she can be on her way, but not before helping the hero discover a way to save the castle after all.'

'She sounds great, if I wasn't marrying Millie, I'd marry her myself.'

'A little moping from the hero before he realises with the help of his sister, his childhood best friend, and his best friend's love interest that he can't let her go and embarks on a mad dash to the airport and a happy ever after.'

'I can't wait to see it. Promise me there will be lots of beautiful shots of Glenmere looking like the perfect Scottish castle, and some walks through forests and around lochs?'

'Promise.'

'One small point, it'll still be October when you start filming, there won't be any snow for at least a month and these things can never be guaranteed, even in the Cairngorms.'

'All taken care of.'

'Intriguing. You'll have to let me know your

secret. Weather on cue is every event professional and every farmer's dream. Do you enjoy it?'

'The fake snow? Not as much as the real thing. No good for sledging or snowball flights...' She stopped abruptly and looking over Charlie saw a tinge of red on her cheeks and he was irresistibly drawn to the memory of the last time he had indulged in a snowball fight with her. He quickly carried on the conversation.

'Not the snow, the job. You don't miss being in front of the camera or on-stage? You were good, as far as my limited knowledge goes. I took Tabby to see you when you were in that musical. Not my kind of thing but you had something, that was obvious even then.'

'My dad always said I was the most talented of the lot of us.' Her colour increased. 'That must sound really big-headed, I don't mean it that way, but in a family like ours...'

'No, not at all. It's a fact, and talent is a thing to celebrate. Tabby is always quick to point out I'm not heir because I am any better than her, just older and with a y chromosome.'

'She may have mentioned that to me once or twice,' Liberty said drily and Charlie laughed.

'I bet she has. I am very grateful she has so far used her considerable talents for the good of the family estate but I don't take them or her for granted.'

'If you and Millie have a daughter first would you break the entail?'

'If me and…?' Charlie remembered his position as a happily engaged man with a jolt. Concentrating on the road, on the two months ahead, enjoying chatting to Liberty, he had, somehow, forgotten his new status. 'We haven't talked… I don't know what Dad…' He stopped and pulled himself together. After all, this putative eldest child was the entire reason for the engagement. 'The problem is that we can't change the title. So, if we break the entail, which I quite agree is old-fashioned beyond belief, sexist and, as Tabby points out, wrong-headed because the matrilineal line is the only one to guarantee continuity…'

'Yes, I have heard her mention that too. Once or twice.'

'Times a hundred? She's right, but although Parliament has acted on the royal line of succession they haven't on hereditary titles. So we can break the entail and then risk separating the estate and title, or we carve the estate up which for the next generation might be fine but in one hundred years might mean it's in pieces too small to support the houses or to make farming worthwhile, hence the need for the entail in the first place.'

'Climate change might mean we are not even

here in one hundred years, or a meteorite might have crashed into us or anything.'

'Cheerful point well made.'

'And does anyone actually need an estate like yours in the twenty-first century let alone the twenty-second? After all, you have the entire family working on keeping it solvent.'

'Another good point, but is it better that we keep the houses in good condition and generally accessible to the public or let them fall into private hands? So much expensive real estate now belongs to people who visit once or twice a year at most. There are the tenants, the farmers, the conservation areas to think of… I'm not saying you don't have a valid argument but it's not quite as easy as just selling it all on or carving it up between all the Howard heirs worldwide. So, for now I'll carry on as we are and look at the entail if it becomes an issue, I suppose.'

'Did you ever mind? Having your future decided for you like this?'

Charlie concentrated on the road ahead. No one had ever asked him that before, assuming that the title and the prestige made up for the lack of autonomy.

'Lots of people in my position spend some years in the city building up their fortune before taking the reins. Giles has been very successful doing just that but it never appealed to me,' he said after a while. 'I'm lucky I guess, there was never anything else I wanted to do. I like the land. I like the opportunities I get to farm or build or wield a chainsaw or dig a ditch. I am proud of the communities we help foster. The people we employ. The business my mother started as a young bride which is now a substantial part of our income. I'm not a natural event planner like Tabby but I can do it if I need to, I'm not a born farmer like so many of our tenants but I am learning all the time, and I trust their expertise. I know I am lucky so, no, I don't hanker over what might have been if I had been born plain Charlie Howard of 10 something road. But how did we get onto me? Nice deflection, Gray.'

Liberty hadn't consciously chosen to move the conversation from her career to Charlie, she was genuinely interested. So much of what she knew of him, thought of him, was coloured by Tabby who didn't go in for subtlety. She liked that he wasn't instantly defensive about his title and privilege but thoughtful about what they represented and meant, the love for the estate he stood to inherit shining through.

'Do I have any regrets? No is the short answer. Not a single one. I always had disgusting stage fright, hate having my photo taken, and find a lot of acting boring.' She laughed at the surprise on Charlie's face. 'This is why my dad says my talent is wasted on me. No, I always preferred backstage, finding out how it all worked, spending time with props or costume or lighting, seeing a play or film come together behind the scenes. I like *doing*, keeping busy. There is a lot of hanging around on film sets, I want to be running around with a clipboard and an earpiece problem-solving, not sitting in a trailer having my make-up touched up, not having started work at 10am despite a 5am call.'

'Sounds reasonable to me. And if the star did get taken ill you could always step in.'

'Unlikely. I'd be too busy placating the anxious property owner, or I'd be one hundred miles away organising the next location shot.'

Liberty's phone rang and she answered it with a murmured apology, noting that Charlie immediately turned the radio down and kept it down as she continued to work throughout the long journey, though he often sang along in a surprisingly decent voice. Tabby, as she knew all too well, was completely tone-deaf but an enthusiastic karaoke partaker regardless.

Charlie's powerful car ate up the miles and they had only had one comfort and coffee break when they reached Newcastle where, instead of following the A1 up the gorgeous coastline

Charlie followed the road inland up to Edinburgh. The scenery was magnificent, getting more beautiful with every mile north but, as it took at least four hours from Newcastle to Glenmere which was situated at the bottom of the Cairngorms, it was a relief when they stopped at a pub in Melrose to stretch their legs and grab a sandwich before the final push.

Seeing Glenmere for the first time was always a breathtaking experience. It seemed to just appear on the horizon, magicked up from the mountains, graceful grey spires surrounded by trees, snow-capped peaks framing the whole. As the car neared other details came into view; the loch, blue and mysterious, the seemingly never-ending pine forests. It was like a scene from a child's storybook, and, she thought with relief, it would look *glorious* on film.

Soon the clocks would change and the nights draw in early, which meant the director would want as many outside shots as possible first, and as Charlie pulled up in the small car park to the side of the castle, she was already calculating where she would recommend they shoot the snow scenes. For the backdrop shots they would use CGI, but for close-ups they would need fake snow, a biodegradable vegetable starch concoction.

Before Charlie had had a chance to switch the

engine off a welcoming committee appeared to meet them, and Charlie jumped out of the car to greet the small group with hugs and handshakes, displaying the natural warm affability that had always characterised him. There was nothing of the heir about him, there never had been. Charlie had a gift for friendship, for putting people at their ease, it was one of the things she had always been drawn to. She got out of the car and joined him, returning the warm smiles with relief. Returning to Glenmere was like coming home.

Charlie indicated a fifty-something woman with a no-nonsense expression and kind eyes. 'Mrs McGregor, you remember Liberty, don't you?'

'Of course,' Mrs McGregor replied in her soft Highlands accent. 'Welcome, my dear. It's good to see you back. Now, Charlie, the family apartment is all ready, but I didn't know where anyone else will be staying and although everything is decorated and furnished there is still a lot to do. You did say I could bring in help from the village…'

'Liberty will be sleeping in the family apartments so no need to worry about anything else for a week at least, but then I am afraid we will be going from nought to hundred. We'll probably need every bed in the castle and all the cottages and lodges. Get all the staff you need, but this is just the start I hope, Mrs M. After this we will be ready for business so start with temps if you must but get recruiting everyone you need.'

The older woman nodded. 'And food? Will the restaurant be open?'

'We haven't employed a chef yet. This has rather caught us on the hop but…'

'There will be catering vans offering three meals and snacks to the cast and crew, so you don't need to worry about that,' Liberty interceded and Charlie nodded.

'But let's get recruiting anyway and if you could find it in your heart to make one of your famous breakfasts now and then you will have my undying love.'

'Oh, get away with you.' But Mrs McGregor couldn't hide her pleasure at the compliment.

'Let Liberty and I have a day to sort out requirements for the next ten weeks or so and then you and I need to look further ahead. But for now, let's get inside where I am sincerely hoping there is tea and maybe some scones awaiting us.' Another flash of that boyish grin.

'Tea and scones indeed. As if I didn't have enough to do with the short notice.' But they were led straight into the library where, despite the mildness of the day, a fire roared and a fresh-looking pot of tea sat on the coffee table next to a plate heaped with still warm buttered scones.

Charlie laughed. 'How do you do it, Mrs M? You must be a witch.'

'Witch indeed. My sister, you remember Morag? She saw you drive by and texted me.'

'I prefer the old days when an owl would deliver the message.' Charlie looked around with a contented sigh. 'Oh it's good to be back.'

'You were only here a month ago,' the housekeeper pointed out.

'True, but a lifetime has passed in that month. You know, when I am in Norfolk, I think there is no more glorious place. The sea and those endless skies. But then I come here to the sheer majesty of the landscape and I think this is the most beautiful place on earth. Have a scone, Liberty, and then I'll show you to your room and give you a quick tour while the daylight lasts. I'm looking forward to seeing what they've done since I was last here. Video calls are all very well but nothing beats seeing it in person.'

'Can I get you anything else?' the housekeeper asked and when, through a mouthful of scone, Charlie assured her that he had everything he wanted and more, she stood for a moment.

'I hope you don't mind me saying how pleased the staff and I, the villagers as well, were to hear about your engagement. Miss Millie is a lovely young woman and we hope you will be very happy.'

For a moment Charlie looked startled, as if he had no idea what Mrs McGregor was taking about, but he quickly recovered himself. 'Thank you. I'm sure she'll be up to visit very soon.'

'It's a long time to be away from her, especially so soon after the engagement,' Liberty said as the housekeeper left them alone with the scones and the fire. 'You must miss her.'

'We both have busy lives so we're used to it. Scone?'

It was definitely a shutdown of the subject. Liberty took one of the temptingly smelling scones and forgot her questions as she took a bite. But once the crumbs were cleared, the tea drunk and their bags carried to their room, she couldn't help reflect that Charlie was behaving less like a newly engaged man and more like a man who had forgotten he had a fiancée at all. He didn't mention Millie every other sentence, wasn't constantly calling her, didn't smile at the mention of her name. It was all very strange, but it was also, she told herself firmly, absolutely none of her business.

CHAPTER SEVEN

LIBERTY WAS RELIEVED that there were enough hours of light left to do a quick tour; she was keen to stretch her legs after the long drive, especially after spending the whole of the previous day at her dining room table. Charlie suggested that he show her one of the newly refurbished cottages so that she could make sure it had everything her crew needed, picking one less than a mile from the castle for the tour.

The air was colder than it had been in London but immeasurably fresher and Liberty took in great lungfuls as she walked along the wide gravel paths, filling her eyes and mind with the landscape, the colours and natural beauty. Not for the first time, she wondered if it was time to leave London. But where would she go? Most of her friends lived in the city and she had no family she would want to settle near.

'I hope the distance isn't going to be a problem,' she said as they walked. 'I know it's just a mile to this one but the lodges and other cottages are a little further away and when people have 5am calls they don't tend to be in the mood for a nice nature walk.'

'I have several golf buggies for getting around the estate, we can get everyone collected, I'll show you the route to the other cottages tomorrow,' Charlie assured her. 'Then you can check out the lodges as well, before we go into the village to discuss rooms with Angus at The Leaping Salmon, although he's already put them all on reserve for you. There are a few hikers and tourists booked in but he's arranged a transfer with the hotel further around the loch at your expense, so hopefully that will be okay.'

'That's very accommodating of him, I'll have to let him know how grateful I am.'

'It's eight weeks' full income versus a night here and there plus the drinks and any food you lot buy. Angus isn't going to let that slip away! Okay, all the cottages are decorated in a sort of modernish but traditional style...'

'Interesting description.'

'Tabby would know the correct terms, but you know what I mean. Anyway, the lodges are a little more modern as they are all newly built, the tree-houses properly traditional with a lot of leather and wood, and the domes super modern, but they all incorporate the same themes using the family colours. You're the first person who's not local or from the estate to see them so I am really interested in your thoughts.'

'And if I hate them?' she teased. 'Will you rip it all out and start again?'

'It was all approved by Tabby and my mother so take it up with them.'

'I wouldn't dare. I am sure I'll love it; anything has to be better than all that oppressive dark wood and that Victorian deep red they were before.'

'Hopefully. Okay, here we are. This one is a two-bed cottage.'

Liberty had always liked the traditional tartan the Howards had adopted from the Scottish three-times-great-grandmother who had bequeathed them the castle, a soft mix of warm greens, misty greys and heathery purples which reflected the Glenmere landscape. As Charlie had promised the cottage took its inspiration from the family colours, the walls a light grey, the sofa upholstered in the tartan with the comfortable looking brown leather chairs heaped with matching cushions. The bedrooms were decorated in a soothing sage-green, the furniture a warm, polished oak, the bathroom luxuriously appointed. Liberty breathed a sigh of relief. Her crew would be more than comfortable here.

'It's gorgeous. I could move in and never leave.'

'Tabs was in charge of briefing the interior designers. Even I have to admit she's done a pretty good job. But you know, cosy as it is, the views are what really makes it stand out.' Charlie gestured towards the sliding glass doors at the back, overlooking a deck with views through the trees to the loch-side. 'Imagine waking up to that.'

'Yes,' Liberty murmured, looking at his profile. 'Imagine.'

There was also time for a tour of the refurbished castle before dinner, the strong patterns and heavy dark mahogany furniture favoured by Charlie's grandmother stripped away once again for the more muted family colours teamed with warm oak. Dinner was taken in the bar rather than the dining room on a small table next to the fire, and they spent the delicious meal discussing the timetable for the next two weeks. Liberty had now spent so much time one-on-one with Charlie that any shyness or anxiety about being alone with him had ebbed away and she found herself falling into the old easy manner. Even sharing an apartment was going to be okay, the space allotted to the family taking up three floors with her bedroom on the first and his on the second, both with en suites, and she would be too busy to use the communal areas much anyway.

But as she drifted off to sleep that night, she couldn't help but reflect again that it was odd how little Charlie mentioned Millie. He wasn't avoiding the topic, her name was mentioned in passing, with affection but not with the kind of intensity she would expect from such a whirlwind romance. He didn't smile goofily when he texted her or disappear off for long intimate conversations. It was all a little odd but it made no difference. He was engaged and out-of-bounds and that suited her just fine.

The next two weeks flew by. Liberty was so busy that, after the full site tour and trip into the village on their first full day, she saw very little of Charlie.

The producer had decided to fly in early, quickly followed by the director, and to her relief both were charmed by the castle. The production designer, key grip and assistant director also arrived earlier than planned, with the rest of the crew due the next day, followed by the cast three days later. It was somewhat of a relief. No more intimate conversations with Charlie, no more analysing his expression as he replied to texts from Millie, no more avoiding a certain walk and a certain tree and certain memories.

She barely saw him in the apartment either. Charlie had arranged with Mrs McGregor that she would supply breakfast and dinner for everyone staying in the castle; the catering vans supplemented by the pub and the self-catering facilities for those staying in lodges and cottages would more than do for everyone else. Charlie had also suggested turning the restaurant into a cafeteria, with the catering vans parked as close as possible with permanent inside coffee and snack stations. 'From what I remember films run on caffeine,' he said. 'And it's soon going to get too cold for people to want to eat outside.' But he usually ate separately in the apartment or at the pub while she dined with the rest of the senior crew.

Not only were their rooms on separate floors but he also had taken to using the study in the turret in his spare time, spending his days travelling around the estate and village, his evenings, she assumed, on paperwork—or binging on reality shows or sport or reading—she never ventured up there to check. She'd gradually taken over the bright, comfortable sitting room as her workspace, her never-ending to-do lists spread over the coffee table. She'd almost forgotten she had a flatmate at all. Almost.

Liberty enjoyed being back at Glenmere. She loved being busy, absorbed in the minutiae of her job, and the change in location meant many extra-long days, working with the director to scope out the best places for outdoor scenes and the scenery, directory and props leads to refit the interior, moving a few rooms around to fit their vision and the need to accommodate cameras and crew. Wires had already been neatly trailed through the house, most of the Howard belongings carefully boxed away with just a few mishaps, and the props for the film hung on the walls. Today, they had started decorating for Christmas. And that must be why she had been aware of a certain melancholy all day. One that seemed to intensify the more garlands and baubles and lights that were hung.

Liberty wasn't a huge fan of Christmas. It was a time when she was always very conscious of not having a home of her own. Oh, she had the flat and she was eternally grateful for that, but Christmas was about returning to familiar places and traditions, about family, and her own lack of all those things felt very stark as December approached. She could go to her mother's, she was always, if not exactly welcome, accepted, but she felt like a stranger there. She wanted to be the bigger person but she found it hard to see the traditions that excluded her, the effort made for this new family that had never been part of her childhood, the matching stockings for each of her siblings, the Christmas Eve boxes, the Boxing Day party, events in which she was an onlooker, not a participant.

She often spent Christmas with Tabby, but this year was Charlie's wedding and not only did she not expect an invite, she didn't want to be around it at all. She told herself that she no longer had a crush on Charlie but couldn't deny that she was still far too drawn to him. So better to keep her distance.

It was a good plan and one she had implemented almost effortlessly thanks to their busy timetables and, she suspected, because he was avoiding her as assiduously as she was avoiding him. So, it was a surprise to head into the boot room that evening on a mission to get some fresh air, and to immediately trip over an outstretched foot. She would have gone headlong if Charlie hadn't caught her, his hands strong on her arms as he broke her fall and set her upright.

'Steady. Do you always hurtle into a room like that?' His blue eyes laughed at her.

'I didn't expect a great big foot to be in my way,' she retorted, aware of his hands still lightly clasping her, the lack of distance between them. She was so close they were nearly touching and she hurriedly took a step back, nearly tripping again.

'Been at the whisky?'

'Ha very ha.' Liberty pulled her scarf firmly around her neck, shoving her hands into her gilet pockets.

Damn it, did he have to be so attractive? Did his eyes have to be so warm and so very blue? Did his hair have to tousle adorably? Did he always have to look as if he was pleased to see her? Did he have to suit autumnal country wear as if he were made for it—although to be fair with his heritage he was. She felt a little like she was playing dress-up in wellies, but Charlie rocked a wax jacket and sturdy boots like the sometime farmer he was. The posh sometime farmer.

'I just fancied some air. It's been an intense couple of weeks, and it's just going to get more intense. You?'

'The final tweaks to the last tree-house were finished today and I wanted to take a look.' He paused. 'Want to come with me or was this a solo mission?'

Liberty glanced at him, trying to gauge if he really wanted her company or was just being polite. She hadn't accompanied Charlie on any of his tours of the estate since the first couple of days; she'd been too busy, plus, there was the whole keeping her distance plan. But she was intrigued by the four tree-houses, whimsical structures hidden in the depths of the Glen-

Of course we could have opened up with just a lick of paint and a refresh, but branching out into full on hospitality beyond a couple of cottages here and there is a new venture for us. We wanted to do it right from the start.'

'I think you can tick that off your list. This is going to sell out, I am sure of it.'

'Let's hope you're right. The photographer is coming next week, and I have a travel marketing expert coming too to advise on the website and PR. It's a good thing I am based up here for now after all. Launching all of this properly is a full-time job. More Tab's expertise than mine but she's happy to boss me from London.'

'I'll bet she is.'

Charlie had a list of things to check, and he busied himself while Liberty looked around, glorying in all the hidden details, the clever workmanship, the effortless-looking luxury, and was sorry when Charlie announced he was done.

'Go without me. I am going to move in, didn't I mention it?'

'I thought you wanted to see the domes?'

'Are they as cool as this?'

'Some might think even cooler…'

'In that case I guess I could tear myself away,' she said reluctantly.

mere forest, like something from a fairy tale suspended high above the floor. 'I might even throw in a trip to the domes,' he added. 'It's going to be a clear night and I haven't tested them properly yet.'

'I haven't even seen the domes,' she said, intrigued. 'Where are they?'

'The other side of the loch. Fancy it?'

Liberty bit her lip. What harm could an evening sightseeing do? Besides, Tabby was bound to demand a review of all the new facilities. 'I'd love to,' she said. 'Let me get my shoes on.'

She followed Charlie round to the car park where he headed for one of several neatly parked golf carts. Liberty climbed into the passenger side and he took off with practised ease.

'I was planning to walk,' he said. 'But if we are getting to see the domes as well then we need some speed. It's always a shock when we get to this time of year and realise daylight isn't a limitless resource.'

Sure enough, the sky was beginning to pinken, the sun low in the sky. 'With sunsets like the ones we've had recently we can't complain,' Liberty pointed out and Charlie nodded.

'Agreed.'

To Liberty's surprise it took less than ten minutes to arrive at the tree-house. For all its air of seclusion it was close to one of the narrow roads which criss-crossed the estate, within a fifteen-minute walk of the village and pub. A twisty spiral staircase descended from the porch two storeys high and Charlie gestured for her to go first.

'Go on, I am really interested in your reaction.'

'Okay.' She was a little nervous as she ascended the staircase but for all its air of fragility it was sturdy with wide planks under her feet. She emerged onto a large wraparound porch that extended across several trees, high railings making it feel safe despite the height. 'Oh, Charlie, this is incredible! The views alone are worth whatever extortionate amount you are charging.' She looked around at the porch swing, the outdoor sofa heaped with blankets, the lanterns creating an intimate glow, the hot tub and outside bar area. 'Is that a sauna?'

'Yup, and the whole place is completely private.' He produced a key and swung the arched door open. 'Come and take a look inside.'

She didn't need a second invitation and stepped in, aware that Charlie was close by her side, watching for her reaction. She didn't have to feign how impressive she found it, the inside as beautiful as the out with its rug-covered wooden floors, high arched ceilings, the way it was luxuriously and sympathetically kitted

out from the central stove to the clever circular seating. Throws, cushions and large paintings brightened the room, relieving the polished wood.

'Oh, Charlie, it's amazing. I want to sink down onto that lounger, light the stove, grab a blanket and a glass of wine and never leave. How many bedrooms are there?'

He couldn't hide his pleasure at her reaction, his smile broad. 'This one has two. We have a smaller one-bedroom especially for couples, two of these and the fourth is a four-bed for larger families or groups of friends. This is the master...' He opened a door to a circular chamber, dominated by a large comfortable-looking bed. An ajar door led into the en suite, a huge bath in the window, a skylight above. 'You can literally bathe surrounded by the forest.'

'Let me move in. Don't we need my room for someone else? I am happy to slum it here. This is gorgeous, Charlie. It's going to be a real draw.'

He rubbed a hand across his face. 'I hope so. I think I said that we went all out here. Glenmere has been a substantial investment. While my grandmother was alive, she didn't want anything changed. The only income was a handful of old-fashioned cottages and forestry and with an estate of this size it just wasn't enough.

'So it's safe to assume you like the tree-houses?' he asked as he locked the door behind them.

'Love them, want them, wish you had had them when I was a teenager. Can you imagine the fun Tabby and I could have had up here?'

'I shudder to think. Carnage, absolute carnage.'

They walked back to the golf cart and this time Charlie took the passenger seat. 'Do you want to drive?'

'I don't know where we are going,' but she was tempted.

'Just follow the path round.'

Liberty hopped in and turned the key. 'So the plan is Glenmere will be more of a traditional holiday destination not just an event hire. Is this a new thing for all your properties or just here?'

'Just here for now, and it will hopefully be a combination of both. The pub and the villagers who work on the estate need more than just a few weddings and photo shoots. There were a lot of meetings, a lot of discussion, a lot of ideas between the village, staff and family. We even considered making the castle a hotel, but decided to keep it for private lets and events, but open up the grounds by adding more luxury accommodation. It's providing jobs, will hopefully do wonders for the economy and attract people to this beautiful corner of Scotland. That's the plan anyway.' His mouth twisted into a rueful smile. 'Otherwise, it's just a hideously expensive folly.'

'I hadn't really thought about it, that you need to innovate and change as you go. Just starting the events business must have felt like such a big thing to do back when your parents married.'

'The hardest part was convincing my grandparents, but it was definitely the right thing to do. We have to remember that we are just the custodians of the land whether that's here or Norfolk. It belongs to nature, to the people who live here through generations. My role is to sustain that in as many ways as I can. It can be a burden sometimes, but then there is an evening like this and it's an absolute joy.'

The sun was really low now, the sky a kaleidoscope of orange and purple and pink lighting up the mountains and reflecting on the lake. With increasing confidence Liberty drove them around the top of the loch until Charlie directed her off onto a narrow path which led to a small clearing by the loch empty apart from a futuristic-looking clear dome with a raised terrace at the front and an enclosed cabin at the back. Liberty pulled up outside it and killed the engine, turning to stare at it fascinated. 'It's not going to take off, is it? It looks like a spaceship.

Are you sure you're not an alien and this isn't an abduction?'

'Not that I am aware of. Want to risk going inside?'

'Only if you promise not to take me to Mars.'

'Promise. I know it looks a little odd but there's no artificial light this side of the loch, so the idea is when you are in one of these domes with the lights off there is no light pollution and, on a clear night, like this promises to be, the stars should be incredible.'

Liberty looked around. 'Where's the other one?'

'About half a mile away. We'll start with two and then if they're popular we'll add more. We only use this side for walks and forestry, so it was just a case of using the natural clearings, improving the access roads and actually building the things. Oh, and installing the domes.'

'Only.'

'Simpler than a tree-house anyway, but equally cool I think. Come take a look.'

Inside the domes were cosy, two deep chairs overlooking the terrace which was complete with a wood-fired hot tub and outdoor wooden sofa. The rest of the dome was dominated by a huge bed, heaped with cushions and blankets. The whole dome was transparent apart from the back wall in which two doors were set, one at each side, leading into a fully kitted-out kitchen on one side, complete with a breakfast bar, and a luxurious bathroom on the other.

It was nearly dark now, a clear night, the first stars peeping out, clearly visible through the glass. 'Wow!' Liberty stared up at the ceiling transfixed. 'This is going to be incredible later on.'

'We can wait for a while if you want?' Charlie offered. 'It's perfect conditions for stargazing.'

Liberty hesitated. There were two chairs, and a comfortable-looking chaise on one side, but it couldn't be denied that there was a love nest vibe about the dome, the bed the dominant feature.

'Or do you have yet another dinner meeting?' Charlie must have noticed her hesitation. 'Do you need to get straight back?'

Get yourself together, Liberty. It's just a bed! 'Not tonight. Simone and Ted have gone to Edinburgh for the evening, the rest of the crew are staying in a hotel there and will be arriving onsite tomorrow so there's a prep session there.' She sank down onto one of the chairs. 'It would be lovely to stay and see the stars.'

'Great, I'll text Mrs M and ask her to put some food in the warmer. You don't mind eating a little later?'

'Last night it was after nine before we got

round to eating. To say it's been busy doesn't come close to describing how insane it has been but I am very grateful to you, Charlie, we all are, and in many ways Glenmere is a better fit for us than the original location.' She laughed. 'Thanks to the renovation it's definitely a lot more luxurious. The crew are going to be delighted with the five-star vibes. But condensing three months of work into two weeks has been a challenge I would have been happier not to have taken on.'

Charlie took the chair next to hers, long legs stretching out. 'It suits you. I can tell you enjoy the adrenaline. You've looked, I don't know, fired up.'

'I have enjoyed it, in a way,' she admitted, both pleased and a little embarrassed that Charlie had noticed. 'But I would prefer most shoots to be more straightforward.' She leaned back and looked up at the sky, now a deep purple, and sighed with satisfaction. 'I love it up here as well, the air is so fresh it completely re-energised me. Obviously, London is great, being able to get out to the best bars and restaurants, to go to the theatre on a whim and stuff like that.'

Charlie grinned. 'And how often do you take advantage of that?'

'Well, hardly ever,' she admitted. 'Ugh. I am

twenty-six and single and I am a workaholic. You're right, I could live anywhere. The two evenings I spent at the local pub here were the most frivolity I have enjoyed for months, except when your sister drags me out.'

'Tabby never lets anything get in the way of her social schedule,' her fond brother agreed.

'She's an inspiration. I know I am lucky to live in such an amazing area, everything walkable or on my doorstep, good transport links, Regent's Park just a stroll away...'

'The zoo.'

'The zoo. Not that I have been there since school, but I could.'

'If you weren't such a workaholic.'

'Exactly. If I lived somewhere like this, I like to think I'd go hiking at weekends, swim in the loch.'

'Now you're romanticising, that loch is icy even in the middle of summer.'

She ignored him. 'Be part of the village community. If it wasn't for Tabby, London would be a little, oh I don't know, lonely I guess. I love my flat, don't get me wrong, but it's easy to be lost in the crowd, and everyone else always looks like they have it sussed. But you're right. I am romanticising. I've been here a fortnight and not managed even one hike. Workaholics are going to work, I guess.'

'How about relationships? Or do you want to follow the template of your film, move to a small town and marry the local laird?'

'Seeing as you're the local laird and off the market it's a good thing that's not my plan.' She felt her cheeks heat. She had meant to make a light joking comment, but instead it had sounded almost wistful. 'One thing the city *is* good for is dating, especially if you're not after anything serious. Which I'm not,' she added firmly. 'Work comes first. Dating is purely a recreational activity.' She told herself that she preferred her love life short, sweet and uncomplicated but she knew part of her was scared to explore anything more meaningful. That rejection felt inevitable, especially from those who should love her, and she had to do all she could to shield herself from it.

'I don't know how you and Tab do it. I enjoy being in the city, for all the reasons you mentioned, I like the buzz of it, and I am lucky to have a central base when I am there, but give me Norfolk and its horizons any time, or here with air that makes you feel alive and landscapes that fill your spirits.'

Their eyes caught and held and Liberty was acutely aware of him, the lock of hair falling over his forehead, the pulse in his neck, the curve of his mouth. She knew them as well as she knew her own face, was attuned to his every shifting mood. She had, after all, fallen in love with him when she was twelve and he had been carelessly kind to her in a way her lonely heart had soaked up.

And she couldn't help but wonder, despite all the many good reasons not to be, whether she was still in love with him.

But she knew better than to think that love equalled a happy ever after.

And he wasn't free.

'Where will you and Millie live?' she blurted out, needing Millie between them, like a shield. 'Norfolk? Or would you settle here, do you think?'

He blinked, as if waking up from an enchantment. 'Live? You know, we haven't really discussed it. Her business is between Norfolk and London so either would work I suppose. I guess I just thought we would move into my apartments there but of course my parents are onsite, as are Aunt Flic and Millie's mum. That's a lot of close relatives to start married life with, even…' He stopped. 'Here would be amazing, but she has a whole business, a client list, I don't think she could be so cut off.'

They hadn't even discussed it. Whirlwind was one thing, but this was the oddest engagement she had ever come across—and she couldn't help thinking that Charlie was hiding something from her. Charlie's love life had nothing to do with her but every instinct told her something wasn't right.

CHAPTER EIGHT

Now why on earth had he asked Liberty about her love life? Things had been working out just the way Charlie had planned. He had been busy, Liberty had been busy, they had barely seen each other the last couple of weeks and that was exactly how he wanted it. Only here he was and here she was, the stars lighting up the sky above them, in an intimate venue orchestrated for romance and rather than keep the conversation to innocuous topics he'd got as up close and personal as possible. Why was he so interested in her personal life? Why did he want to know what made her tick? To be the one to make her eyes light up with laughter, to make her smile, to feel the connection between them?

Because there was a connection. An undeniable palpable connection. Charlie was still attracted to her, and that attraction seemed to deepen every day. But he couldn't act on it, *mustn't* act on it. Millie might have given him a get-out-of-jail card but it couldn't include Liberty. She was too close. There was history between them. There was emotion. And none of that added up to a last-minute fling but to mess and drama and everything he didn't want and she didn't deserve.

Liberty leaned back, staring up at the roof. The chairs were designed so users could stare up at the domed roof and out at the stars. There were more now, he saw as he tilted his head up, so much brighter than ever seen in London or even at Howard Hall.

The lighting in the dome was low, to enable the stars to be seen, a dull light strip along the bottom of the walls made it possible for occupants to make their way around the room without bumping into furniture or each other. Cast just enough light for him to see Liberty's elegant outline, the fall of her hair, the curve of her body, but not her expression.

'Tabby is so happy for you,' she said, almost wistfully. There had always been a wistful quality to Liberty. On the surface she had it all, money, famous parents, looks, talent, but he would see her at games nights, at Christmas, watching their family interactions, her eyes sad, loneliness running through her. It made him want to pull her close, to assure she was wanted, loved, but of course it wasn't his place.

His mother, he knew, had and did. She even called her *her other daughter*, a joke but one with truth behind it.

'I think she's convinced herself it's all down to her?'

Liberty's laugh was bell-like, clear and warm. 'How exactly?'

'Details are not forthcoming. Apparently, she had a feeling that Millie and I were perfect together and that was enough for her to claim full credit.'

'Sounds like Tab.' She paused. 'How about you? When did you know? I didn't see…at the wedding…but of course you…'

'You mean when did Millie and I…' Charlie wanted to say *fall in love* but he couldn't form the words. 'Hold on, I just want to check something.'

It really was dim now and Charlie was grateful for the low lighting as he edged his way around what really was an all-dominating bed—had he created romantic stargazing pods or just giant shag palaces—and into the kitchen. All accommodation would be supplied with hampers and any additional requests whilst being prepared, but he had suggested that they were kept stocked with staples which should include…he opened the fridge. Oh yes! Champagne. For one moment he wondered if adding alcohol into the already overwrought mix was a good idea, but he pushed the thought away. Champagne was always a good idea. The cupboard yielded up a large bag of locally made gourmet crisps and he tipped them into a bowl, grabbed two glasses, put the bottle into an already frozen ice bucket and made his way back to the front of the pod.

'I thought you might be in need of refreshment seeing as we are delaying dinner.'

'Oooh, champagne. As diversion techniques go this is a good one.'

'Diversion technique?' As if he didn't know. Charlie opened the bottle and poured two generous glasses before setting the ice bucket on the table between them and handing her a glass.

'Cheers. To *Jingle Bell Highlander.*'

'To happy cast and crew, good ratings and sticking to our schedule.' Liberty took a sip and eyed him from over the top of her glass. 'By diversion technique I mean you don't talk much about the wedding, or the engagement or even Millie.'

Charlie didn't answer for a long moment. Coming to Scotland, burying himself with all the work on the estate, was a way of escaping. He had no regrets about his decision to marry Millie, he still knew it was the right thing to do, but the subterfuge didn't come naturally to him. It would all be easier once they were settled into married life, with none of the expectations that came with a whirlwind engagement.

'I guess that's because my relationship with Octavia seemed to dominate every occasion, every conversation. I don't want to make the same mistake twice. Some things are better off private.'

It was Liberty's turn to fall silent. 'I'm sorry,' she said after a while. 'I didn't mean to pry.'

Damn it. Now he had upset her. 'I'm still getting used to it,' he said honestly. 'I didn't think we were going to announce it so soon, or to settle on a date and everything. But once Tabby got involved the whole thing turned into a runaway train and all I can do is cling on and hope to get to my destination intact.'

'That's Tabby! I won't go on, I promise. I get you want to keep part of it for yourself, but I just wanted to say I'm glad you're happy. I don't know Millie super well, but she's always seemed really nice. Genuine. And the two of you have always been so tight, Tabby is right, you are obviously made for each other.' There was that wistful note again, the one that made him want to sweep her into his arms and promise her that everything would be okay. Or maybe just sweep her into his arms. He took a hasty gulp of his drink.

'I first met Millie when I was about four and

she must have been three. Her parents had just arrived at Howard Hall, and she was in the kitchen garden playing, her father was digging and keeping an eye on her. I swaggered up to her with all the dignity of an older boy and announced that the whole garden belonged to my daddy and one day it would belong to me too, and I waited for her to pay homage to me.'

'How very Henry the Eighth of you.'

'She put her little fists on her hips, tilted her chin and told me that her mother knew how to make fifty different types of cake and she had tried them all, and that her father could name every plant in the world. She then went back to her game and ignored me completely for about one minute which lasted a lifetime, then asked if I wanted to play. That was it. We were best friends and stayed that way even when I went to boarding school and then university, even with Octavia always jealous as hell that I was such close friends with another female.'

'Did she have any reason to be?'

'Jealous?' Charlie laughed, forgetting for a moment his status as a head-over-heels fiancé. 'Not at all, Millie and I never had as much as a moment.'

'Until now?' There was a slightly questioning note in her voice. God, he was bad at this!

It was a good thing he was hundreds of miles away from his mother and sister.

'Until now.' He still felt uncomfortable about the thought of any kind of *moment*. It was something he needed to get over fast. The wedding was barely two months away, and Millie deserved a groom who showed some enthusiasm, not embarrassment.

'Do you think if you and Octavia hadn't got together, you and Millie might have done so earlier?'

The honest answer was no. Maybe they might have had a drunken fumble at some point, although he doubted it. But this was a time when honesty definitely wasn't the best policy. Especially as the only relationship he regretted not having the opportunity to pursue was with the woman sitting opposite him, a mere shadow now in the starlit dark. He caught himself. Regret? Was *that* what he felt? He liked Liberty, of course he did. He couldn't deny the attraction he felt for her. Couldn't deny the guilt he felt, the way it must have seemed that he had used her although his only thought back then had been to protect her. But did that mean that he wished he had chosen differently? Wondered what life would have looked like if he'd taken that path?

'It's impossible to say. For better or worse, Octavia is my past.' He hesitated. There was something he had wanted to say for a long time but never had. 'I owe you an apology.'

'Me? Why?' Liberty sounded wary.

'For that New Year's Eve.'

'Oh, Charlie, that was a lifetime ago. It was a drunken kiss. I'd finished school, was all grown up, you have nothing to apologise for.'

'I'm not apologising for the kiss. It was…' He knew he shouldn't say the next words but somehow they were out before he could recall them. 'It was one of the loveliest kisses of my life. I can still see you, in the snow and moonlight…' She was very still, her body tilted towards him. 'No, it's what happened after I need to apologise for. I had no idea Octavia would just turn up. I mean, who heads from London to Scotland on Hogmanay evening like that?' It was a rhetorical question and Liberty didn't answer. She still hadn't moved, even her breathing had slowed. 'But I shouldn't have left you as if that moment, as if you had meant nothing. But Octavia was jealous, could be vindictive. I didn't want her turning her sights onto you.'

'If she hadn't married Layton would you two have ended up getting married instead? You were engaged, after all.'

'No.'

'You sound very sure.'

'I am.' Charlie hesitated. There were things

about Octavia he had never told anyone, not even Millie. 'The thing about Octavia… She's more vulnerable than she lets on. In her family looks, success, money, winning, they are the things that count. Happiness isn't even in the running. Once you understand that it's easy to understand her, to pity her even, although she would be horrified if she thought she was an object of pity. For a long time, I thought I could be the one to save her…' He picked up his glass and realised with some surprise it was empty. He reached for the bottle and topped up first his and then Liberty's. 'But she didn't want saving. She liked the games and the drama. And so, I ended it, this time for good.'

Finally, Liberty moved, a start of surprise. '*You* ended it? But I thought…'

'Everyone thought. Thinks.'

'You don't mind?'

'What difference does it make to me? I don't really care what people think. Besides, over the years she probably instigated more break-ups than I did, she liked me to win her back, so we are probably even. But Layton also likes the game. I'm not sure marrying Octavia would have been so sweet if he didn't think he'd won.'

'They deserve each other.'

'Maybe.' He stared out at the starlit darkness. 'It wasn't easy. I was so used to being in love with her, it felt like it defined me, she defined me. For a long time I really thought we crazy kids would be able to sort things out. But one day I realised that was the last thing she wanted, and the only thing I could do was get free. To set her free to be whatever she wanted. Which wasn't settling down to take on the responsibilities of a huge estate and work in the family business.'

'At the wedding you seemed... I don't know, sad. Heartbroken. Was it all an act?'

'To start with, a little, but of *course* I was genuinely sad. I was saying goodbye to nearly fourteen years, to the future I had once envisioned, to the world in which we were Charlie and Octavia, for better and worse. I might have been the one to make the break but it still hurt. The booze didn't help either. Made me sentimental.' He grimaced. 'Still, it played into the narrative, didn't it? I was the love-lost swain and Layton the victor.'

'Yet all the time you and Millie were together. You are more devious than I gave you credit for.'

'Not all the time.' How much champagne had he drunk? He shouldn't be giving away clues like that. No wonder he hadn't been tapped by the Secret Service when he finished university. He tipped back and looked up. 'Look at the stars, Liberty. Aren't they glorious?'

'Yes.' Her voice was soft. 'They really are.'

* * *

They were, so bright it almost hurt. She reclined the chair the better to see them, all too aware of the huge bed just behind them, her mind sorting through his words looking for clues, she didn't know for what. Trying not to let her mind linger on the soft caress of his voice when he had said how lovely their kiss had been. Trying not to let herself think that it really had been the best kiss of her life.

'How does Millie feel about taking on the estate, producing a dozen mini-barons to carry on the family name?' It was like poking a tongue in a hole in a tooth. Each time it twinged, but she needed to remind herself it was there. Had to remind herself that Charlie was engaged.

'Millie wants a large family so the mini-barons part will be fine. How she'll fit in with the estate, that's another thing TBC. I don't expect her to give up her business. She's worked too hard to build up her reputation. But she grew up at Howard Hall too, she knows what it takes to keep it going. She's coming into this with her eyes wide open.'

'Of course.' There was a *lot* still TBC for a wedding taking place so soon. Of course, the whole thing had been a whirlwind but it seemed like they had made no plans at all. Almost as if the engagement had taken them by surprise…

They hadn't discussed living arrangements, jobs, had allowed Tabby to take over the wedding, although to be fair nobody could stop Tabby once she had set her sights on something. Charlie barely seemed to even remember Millie, let alone miss her. Liberty couldn't shake the feeling that she was missing something, something important.

Not that it was any of her business.

She raised her glass. 'To you and Millie. To drama-free happiness.'

Keep saying it and she might mean it. No, she did mean it, she really wished them both well. She just couldn't wrap her head around them as a couple.

'And here's to you, Liberty Gray. To…what is it you want?'

'We already toasted to that, a smooth shoot, no overrunning, a happy cast and crew and great ratings.'

'No, that's the film, what do *you* want?'

How could she answer that? The truth was she tried hard not to want anything. That way she wasn't disappointed. 'Travel, adventures, fabulous wealth and many exotic love affairs with dangerous men, of course.'

'You don't have to pretend with me, Liberty.'

I'm not pretending…but the words wouldn't

come. Instead, she blurted, 'To come first. For someone to put me first.'

'That should be a given. It's the least you deserve.'

'Maybe. I doubt I am even top five with either of my parents, barely register with my siblings…there's Tab of course, but she has her family, other friends, her dates. One day one of those will turn into something more serious…' She stopped. No more. 'Listen to me being all emo. I'm in this beautiful place, doing a job I adore. I have no right to moan about anything. But talking of jobs, I've another busy day tomorrow. I'd better get back, eat dinner and get some sleep.'

'Of course. Leave those,' as she made a move to pick up the glass and bottle. 'I'll swing by tomorrow to tidy and replace the crisps and champagne. Can you see okay?'

'Fine, thank you.'

Charlie stood up and stood back to let her go past. The space was small, and she had no choice but to brush past him, her body tingling at the brief touch. She stopped and looked back. 'Thank you, by the way.'

'For what?'

'For the apology. I know I said you didn't need to say anything, but I really appreciated it. And for saying that the kiss was lovely. I thought it was but I was quite a naïve eighteen-year-old for all I thought I knew it all. I was a naïve eighteen-year-old with a huge crush, and the kiss meant something to me, although I knew it shouldn't, that it didn't mean anything to you.' Oh. God. *Stop talking, Liberty.*

'I never said it didn't mean anything.' His voice was very low, reverberating straight through her. What she should do was walk through the door and insist she needed some night air and to walk the five kilometres around the loch and back to the castle. What she should do was keep her distance from Charlie Howard for the rest of his natural born life. But her feet wouldn't move. She stood still, acutely aware of him behind her, breathing a little faster, every nerve alive in the dark, starlit space.

She waited.

'It was lovely. It was the sweetest, most genuine kiss I had ever experienced. Have ever experienced. And if Octavia hadn't turned up when she did…'

'Yes?'

'I have often wondered just where that kiss would have taken us.' His voice was silk, wrapping around her senses. 'Would we have stepped apart and pretended it had never happened?'

'It was too cold to go much further where we were.'

'Oh I don't know, we were generating enough heat.'

Walk away, Liberty. Don't turn around.

But of course she was going to turn around. It was easier in the dark, his features hidden, hers equally inscrutable to him. He wouldn't be able to see the need and want that were surely blazing in her eyes, and in the dark she could pretend that he was hers, put her scruples to one side for just a few moments. One step and she was close to him, looking up at him as his hand unerringly found hers, his fingers slipping through hers as if he were made to fit her.

'Liberty Gray,' he murmured. Just two words but there was want in those syllables. Hunger. Need. Feelings that were as intoxicating to her as her own yearning for him thrumming through her body with every increasingly fast beat of her heart. Her whole body was aware of him, the touch of his hand on hers radiating out, creating sweet aches low in her belly, in her breasts, her thighs, aches that intensified as his other hand came to rest on her hip, possessive and yet light.

It wasn't too late. She could, she should still walk away. It was the right thing to do. But couldn't she, just once, do something just for her? What harm could one little kiss do? Liberty had no idea who moved first, but less than a second later his mouth was on hers, Charlie Howard was kissing her for the second time in her life and it was just as glorious as she had remembered.

The amount of tension in the room might have culminated in some kind of passionate explosion, a fierce, all-encompassing kiss, but instead Charlie kissed her like they had all the time in the world, slow, sweet, reverent. Like she meant something. His hand stayed entwined with hers, his fingers caressing the back of her hand in a way that made her knees weaken, and she pressed close to him, holding onto his shoulders like he was all that stopped her being swept away, acutely aware of his other hand resting so lightly on her hip, so tantalisingly close to all the parts of her aching for him. She pressed closer still, glorying in the hard planes of his body next to hers, allowing her hands to wander over his shoulders, his neck, to tangle into his hair, feeling his own clasp on her tighten as he pulled her into position, as he finally moved his hand from her hip, cupping her bottom, pressing her closer until they were both gasping.

The bed was right there. Inviting, romantic, so very close. It wouldn't take much to move there, just a few steps, to sink onto it, to start pulling at clothing, exploring bodies, to touch and be touched, kiss and be kissed, to give in to what they both wanted…

But he wasn't hers to kiss. He wasn't hers to touch.

With a gasp Liberty tore herself away, instantly cold as she stepped back, her every instinct telling her to carry on, that he was hers for the taking, tonight at least.

'We shouldn't have done that.' Her voice was unsteady and she reached out to the wall for support.

'No.'

'I'm sorry.' She was glad she couldn't see his face, that he couldn't see hers, probably raw with need and sorrow.

'Don't be sorry, Liberty. I'm not.'

'But Millie! You're engaged!' She needed to remind herself as much as him.

'I know.' He sounded weary now. 'It's not… it's not quite what you think. I wish I could say more but…' He sighed. 'I think we should get back. Are you okay with the buggy in the dark? I might walk.'

'That might be better. I'll be fine.'

Keep saying it, keep thinking it and it might actually be true.

CHAPTER NINE

IT WAS IN many ways a relief that work didn't let up for either of them and that both Charlie and Liberty were so busy that over the next few weeks they barely had a chance to mumble a hurried and never not embarrassed greeting at each other. The film was in full swing, the castle transformed into either a Christmassy wonderland or kitsch overload depending on your taste. Charlie veered towards the latter, but as long as the Gainsborough was safely in storage in Edinburgh, no one sat on, slept in or did anything other than look at Queen Victoria's bed and all the damage was repaired, then he was happy.

No, happy was not quite the word. Perturbed might be more accurate, restless, guilty. Not because of Millie, although he couldn't decide whether he should mention the kiss to her. They had made an agreement after all, and he really wasn't bothered who she had been kissing over the last few weeks. In fact, he hoped she was kissing lots of people, in a safe and respectfully consensual way of course.

No, he felt guilty for once again dragging Liberty into his emotional dramas. He knew he needed to apologise but look where the last belated apology had got him, right back where they started. He wanted to blame the moment on the stars and the seclusion and the champagne but he knew none of those were the reason why they had kissed. It was because he was drawn to her, attracted to her, wanted her. And she deserved better. What had she said? She wanted to come first with someone. And all he could offer was a paltry second best. A last fling before he settled down. It was unthinkable.

So, it was a good thing she was busy and he equally so. Operation market the hell out of the castle had started in earnest. He'd had the foresight to get a photographer in before the set designers had turned the castle into their clichéd idea of a perfect Scottish castle and the crew had strewn the cottages and lodges with their belongings, and was busy working with web designers, marketing and advertising agencies to create the perfect website and booking experience, to decide which third parties to list with and to reassess the pricing strategy. In addition to all this he was taking advantage of his extended stay to work through the whole estate and forestry management plan. It all meant early mornings, long days and working late into the night. He fell exhausted into bed every night, but still found it hard to sleep. The memory of Liberty's body pressed to his, the feel of the curve of her hip, the taste of her, the way she had held onto him, kept him tossing and turning into the small hours. It didn't help that she was just a floor away. Sometimes he fancied he could hear her breathe, pictured her lying there, her auburn hair spread over the pillow before berating himself for being an idiot and opening his laptop to work some more and carry on with his grown-up plan to keep avoiding her.

The forecast was clear and bright for the next few days, if cold with the first frost of the year turning the air distinctly wintry. Now they were heading into November the leaves had fallen, leaving the trees bare against the skyline and the director decided to take advantage of the forecast to shoot some outside scenes. As Liberty had said, most of the snow would be added later thanks to green screens and other industry tricks Charlie didn't really understand, but for the close-up scenes fake snow was being generated in bulk. Some of the scenes in question involved several extras and to Charlie's horror, the director had asked him to take part, making it clear she thought she was bestowing a great honour.

'No, no, I am much happier behind the camera,' he had protested but to no avail. He, most of the village children, and several much more willing local amateur thespians had been pulled into hair and make-up at an obscenely early hour, kitted out in huge coats that were far too warm for the actual temperature but would come in handy if he ever embarked on an arctic trek, hats and scarves.

Being an extra meant a lot of waiting around and being moved from spot to spot like a piece on the chessboard but to his surprise Charlie quite enjoyed the experience. It was fascinating to see how the leads changed the second the cameras started rolling, instantly becoming their characters, the sincerity they gave their words. The first scene involved the moment the lead actress realised she was snowed in, the second an entire village enjoying sledging followed by a snowball fight. The actual sledging was to be filmed off-site at an indoor slope on the outskirts of Edinburgh, but there were plenty of shots of children tumbling off sledges and the hero and heroine looking into each other's eyes and laughing in a way that made Charlie's chest ache.

Good grief, he was getting sentimental in his old age.

The fake snow was still on the ground when the crew finally packed up, the children were sent back to the village and the cast returned to their rooms to wash the sticky stuff out of their hair. Charlie had gladly relinquished his borrowed coat and hat back to the wardrobe department as he headed down the stairs, where the set designers were indulging in yet more re-arranging, including a few of the castle's own belongings they had begged to be able to use. Charlie was about to remind them to be extra careful with the large and particularly hideous gold vase they were trying to place when his phone rang. Giles.

Of course, he and Millie were at Howard Hall today to discuss guest lists and Charlie really should have phoned in. He didn't think being press-ganged into being an extra would stand up as an acceptable excuse for missing such an important wedding planning moment.

He accepted the call, leaning against the pan-elled wall, his heart beating faster as he saw Liberty, elegant in jeans and a cashmere green jumper, stop to talk to the set advisers who were still tweaking the décor, including the few How-ard belongings Charlie hadn't had put into stor-age. 'How's it going?'

'I think we've managed to persuade your mother and sister to keep the guest list under a thousand or so. But you may now have a twelve-course tasting menu wedding breakfast as a result.' Giles sounded exhausted. Not surprising after a negotiation with Charlie's mother and sister. A negotiation Charlie really should have been involved in.

He groaned. 'Is Millie okay?'

'Your mother is talking to her about wedding gowns and heirloom rings.'

Charlie closed his eyes. He had said he would handle the rings and dresses were definitely not the groom's family's territory. 'I should be there.'

'Trust me, I would definitely rather you were here than me,' Giles said. 'And I'm sure Millie would too.' His pause was so loaded Charlie could envision him, jaw set, eyes blazing with accusation. 'Why aren't you?'

'This movie, up here in Scotland, I need to be here. For the…antiques. Insurance purposes. You know?'

What *was* he babbling about? There were marketing considerations, estate business matters, recruitment too…and it could all be done from Norfolk. The truth was he *wanted* to be here.

In many ways his disappearing act had worked a little too well. He had definitely found it all too easy to put his impending nuptials and the huge changes that awaited him out of his mind most of the time, although every video call with Millie reminded him just how much of the burden she had ended up shouldering, just to add to his guilt. But the downside was he was painfully unprepared for married life. It was November now, which meant his wedding was next month.

It felt so soon. Too soon. But his reasons for marrying Millie were still absolutely valid. He did need an heir, did crave stability and, he reminded himself, there were very good reasons why Millie needed him too. Besides, left to his own inclinations he couldn't be trusted not to let drama overwhelm his love life. Just look at what had happened in the dome.

And with that he was back where he started. Avoiding Liberty, keeping his calls to Millie brief and businesslike and wondering what the hell was wrong with him. He had finally sorted his life out. Why was he so hell-bent on sabotage?

And now his other best friend was annoyed with him—and in turn he had guilt about Giles to add to his long list. When he had asked his friend to step in for him, he thought he might need to help with some cake eating here, maybe some wine tasting there; after all, Tabby and his mother had things under control. But it seemed that Millie was taking on far more of the organising than he had anticipated and Giles was by her side every step of the way. Without too many clashes either, despite their different characters, which was of course great, he'd always wanted his two best friends to get along. In fact, once Charlie had hoped that they might…but of course Giles was wedding averse and Millie was marrying *him*.

A sudden thought struck him, and his hand tightened on the phone. Was Millie sowing her wild oats with *Giles*? She'd been asking questions about him recently, about his background, his parents, the only time their conversation veered away from tulle and colour schemes. And Giles was being *particularly* abrupt. And he had been interested in Millie at Octavia's wedding.

Giles and Millie. It would complicate things. But surely one of them would have said if they were more than bride and best man. He was probably just imagining things. Projecting his own guilt over his attraction to Liberty.

'Right. Insurance.' Yep, there was definitely accusation in Giles's voice. He didn't buy Charlie's reasons for one minute and no wonder. It wasn't as if Charlie was stuck on the other side of the world. He could easily have got back for a day or two if he wanted.

'Tell Millie I'm really sorry she's having to do this alone.' Charlie was about to say more, to apologise again, when there was a shout, some swearing and the ominous sound of a crash behind him. He whirled around, to see his grandmother's favourite vase lying in pieces on the ground, the set designer, dresser and Liberty standing around it, all three staring at him in horror. 'Sorry, I'm going to have to go. Liberty!' He pocketed his phone and waited for an explanation from the guilty-looking group.

'Charlie, I am so sorry. We'll replace it.' Liberty looked tired, her hair pulled back into a ponytail, and there were deep shadows under her eyes.

'I doubt it.' He walked towards them. 'It's Victorian.'

'I know your grandmother loved it.'

'She did, she really did.' He looked down at the shards. 'It was really ugly though.' He smiled at the still horrified set designer. 'You have the insurers' details? Good, I'll let them sort it out.'

He headed for the door, only to turn as he heard footsteps hurry after him. He turned to see Liberty. 'I just wanted to say again how sorry I am. You entrusted us with your house. I know we shouldn't have moved that vase.'

'*I* should have put the vase in storage. The only person who liked it was Grandma and if she's planning to haunt us she will have started by now. She's probably so disgusted by all the renovations she hasn't wanted to hang around. So you can sleep safely.'

'I loved your grandmother. I would be very happy to be haunted by her.'

Charlie smiled. 'She was the best. Honestly, don't worry, Aunt Flic will be sad but we'll cope. We have many other hideous vases.'

One good thing about the toppling of the vase was that it had got him out of the call with Giles, although he did now need to call his mother and remind her that she was to leave rings to him and dresses to Millie. Which meant he needed to actually order the wedding rings as he had promised to do, although he was going to suggest that Millie pick her own engagement ring if she didn't want any of the heirlooms—he didn't blame her if she didn't, hideous overly bling things most of them were. There was that art deco emerald, but it wasn't Millie somehow. Liberty now…

Liberty smiled. 'Thank you for being so understanding. Look, I'm glad I caught you.'

'You are?' *Please don't mention what hap-*

pened because then I'll have to apologise and then it will be out there and there is a lot to be said for keeping things buried.

She looked down at her feet and then seemed to square her shoulders. 'Erm, yes. I just wanted a chance to go over the shooting schedule with you, if you have a chance? We want to do the indoor scenes from next week, which means more upheaval, I appreciate. We're planning to finish as much of the outdoor over the next few days while the weather holds and then start with the castle, then the pub and finally the village hall.'

'Great.' Shooting schedules. Safe, professional, no lips involved. Excellent.

'So, do you want to see the schedule? They are very keen on shooting in Queen Victoria's room but have promised not to touch the bed, I just want to make sure there is nothing else we need to be careful of and check if there are any extra forms to sign.'

Charlie really shouldn't have thought about lips because now he was far too aware of the curve of Liberty's full mouth. He was dimly aware that she was waiting for an answer and managed to pull himself together. 'I think that room is fine but I'll take another look just to be on the safe side. And yes, probably makes sense to go through the schedule too.'

'Great, I was about to head over to The Leaping Salmon to check with Angus. Do you want to come and we can discuss there, or shall we meet later? You can tell me about your acting debut too. Simone said you were a natural.'

Charlie hesitated. Was heading to the pub with Liberty wise? But it was a public space, filled with crew and villagers. What harm could a drink and a chat do?

'Pub sounds great,' he said. 'Let me get my coat and I'll walk over with you.'

It was funny how, despite her vows to stay far away from Charlie and to be nothing but professional when she did see him, Liberty soon fell into her old comfortable way of being with him. It was because she *felt* comfortable with him. Too comfortable. That was why she kept forgetting herself. Getting too close.

But there was no constrained atmosphere as they walked the fifteen minutes across the estate to the pub. Charlie told her some amusing anecdotes about his day on set as an extra and she filled him in on the affair between the actress playing the best friend and the lead actor and the ongoing feud between the set designer and the lead prop designer. He laughed in all the right places, giving her his full attention in a way that warmed her through. It was so unusual these days when most people were connected to at least two devices even during a conversation; she was guilty of it herself, but not Charlie. He was always very present.

The pub, like the castle, was decorated in a set designer's idea of a Scottish Christmas, which meant huge red tartan bows and garlands over everything. At least, Angus said, he didn't need to bother redecorating and as they slipped into November, the decorations looked less odd and just extra.

The pub belonged to the Glenmere estate and, as compensation for the long renovation which had eaten into what little tourism they had, the Howard Estate had paid for a refurbishment of the pub. Nothing too drastic, Charlie told her that they hadn't wanted to incite a village revolt, but a clean-up and repaint, new scrubbed oak tables, reupholstering of benches and chairs, opening up the function room and redecorating the bedrooms. But the fire still crackled in the same 500-year-old hearth, the ceilings were still the same, low and beamed and whitewashed, the same tempting array of single malts were displayed behind the bar. Liberty approved. She always felt at home here, no matter how much time elapsed between her visits.

'My favourite location manager,' Angus proclaimed as they walked in. 'Liberty, if you can bring me a booking like this every year I will be forever in your debt. February would be a good time. Let us recover from Hogmanay but help us manage over the quiet time.'

'I'll bear that in mind,' Liberty promised. She slid into the booth nearest the fire and sank onto one of the now comfortable benches. She might not like too much change but new upholstery was something she did approve of. 'And would you like to have a role in every one of these films?'

'I can't help it if the camera loves me,' he said with a grin. 'What will I get you?'

'Coffee for me, this is a work meeting,' she said firmly. She needed her wits about her if she was going to be dealing with Charlie. Busy and professional, that was the key. That way her mind wouldn't keep returning to the dome, to the secrets he had told her, secrets he hadn't even told his fiancée, to the way her body had swayed towards his, the kiss, even more magical than the first.

No thinking about kissing. He wasn't hers to kiss.

They went over the schedules in some detail, Liberty promising to make sure no more wires were trailing near valuable if ugly vases, before moving over to discuss the next week with Angus. She returned to the table where Charlie was glaring at his phone, and started to tick things off on her iPad.

'The hall is all ready for us to use for the nativity scene, the airport scenes were done before they got here...'

'I always find it odd how films are shot out of order,' Charlie said. 'They did the happy ever after before they had even met. At least with a play you start at A and end up at Z, a film is like alphabet spaghetti.'

'I know. Yesterday we filmed her arrival, today she got snowed in and fell in love, tomorrow she will leave, and then we do the bits in between. But the actors seem to manage.'

'What did you prefer, stage or film?'

'For acting? Stage for all the reasons you said, but I wanted to work on films because it gives me the opportunity to travel. I like spending a few weeks in different places.' She looked over at the fire and sighed in contentment. 'Although right now I feel like I could settle here forever. Sometimes I think Glenmere is the most beautiful place in the world.'

'You're not wrong. I might get a quote from you for the website.' His smile was too intimate and Liberty sat back, wanting some space between them.

'How's Millie?' It felt safer to deliberately bring the conversation around to his fiancée.

'Were you on the phone to her earlier? How's the wedding planning going.'

Charlie looked over to the bar and signalled to Angus, and in just a few moment pints were set in front of them along with an assortment of crisps. Millie looked at Charlie in surprise.

'If we are going to talk weddings I need sustenance,' he explained.

'That bad? I suppose three months *is* a short time to organise a wedding in even with a confirmed venue and professional planners in the family.'

'Maybe I was being ridiculously naïve but I didn't think that I would be leaving Millie—and it turns out, Giles—with so much to do. In my head we were going to do something small and intimate, that we would just turn up at the local church, then head to The Fox and Duchess... *What?*'

Liberty set her pint down and stared at Charlie in amusement. 'The Fox and Duchess? Have you *met* your mother and sister?'

'They are not the ones getting married.'

'No, *you* are. Charles St Clare Howard, heir to one of the oldest baronies in the entire country and just as importantly CEO of a business that relies on showcasing just how ideal his properties are for events such as society weddings.

As if they were going to let you get away with the local pub!'

'I said I was being a little naïve. Okay,' as Liberty raised her eyebrows meaningfully. 'A lot naïve. At least Giles helped Millie battle the guest list down from everyone my parents have ever met to something manageable, but they had to agree to a twelve-course tasting menu in return. If I had been there...'

His voice trailed off.

Of course, he wanted to be there, supporting his bride-to-be, not stuck in Scotland with his sister's best friend who pounced on him whenever she had the opportunity. If she was Millie, she would be furious that Charlie had disappeared for so long at such a crucial time. Liberty took a deep breath. 'Look, you being here is a huge help, but I didn't expect you to be on hand the *whole* time. I'm sure if you needed to head back for a few days or even longer, we could manage.'

'And leave you with the vases unattended?'

'I think you left that vase there on purpose. I'm serious, Charlie, if Millie needs you on hand, then of course you should go home.'

He rubbed his forehead. 'Truth is I had no idea how much Mills was going to take on. I thought she would leave it all to Tabby.'

'Tabby certainly has lots of ideas.' Ideas she sent to Liberty in exhausting detail.

'But it turns out Millie wants some control over the day.'

'And that's a surprise?'

'Under the circumstances...' He stopped, an appalled look on his face. 'Due to how short a time we have, I mean. And now Giles is involved, sending me reminders to pick out wedding rings, addressing the invitations for goodness' sake. It's all such a circus.'

'It's a wedding. It comes with the territory.'

'It wouldn't for you though. At Octavia's wedding you said you wanted something small and intimate.'

He'd remembered? She'd assumed he had been too drunk to remember much of anything they had discussed that night. But then again, he'd not been too drunk to get engaged.

She stared at her still untouched pint, a nagging sense that something didn't add up about his engagement resurfacing. 'Well, in the unlikely event I did get married the alternative would be all ten of my siblings as bridesmaids and groomsmen, Mum and Dad fighting over which magazine to sell the photos to, Dad walking me down the aisle as if he had been part of my life. Ugh.' She shuddered. 'But it's not my wedding. It's yours and Millie's.'

'Right now, it's Mother and Tabby's and Millie and Giles's wedding. Not that I am complaining, I appreciate Giles stepping in and I know the day means a lot to Mum and Tabs.'

She stared at him. 'And to Millie and to you.'

'Right.' He took a long drink. 'Right. I guess I do only get married once. Might as well do it right.'

'Charlie.' The words slipped out before she could stop them. 'Do you actually *want* to get married.'

He didn't answer for a long time. 'I want to settle down, to be married, to have a calm quiet life. I could do without the big day and all the fuss, but you're right. It's not just about me. It's about the title and the estate and the business…'

'And Millie.'

'Right, and Millie.'

If she hadn't kissed him, would she be so interested, so sure that there was a mystery here? She should leave well enough alone, get on with her job and count down the days until she returned to London and Charlie Howard was out of her life. She slid a glance over at Charlie, who was staring into his pint, forehead creased, looking less like an eager groom and more like a man with all the weight in the world weighing him down and knew, that sensible as walking away might be, she just couldn't. She had to find out what was going on.

'Charlie,' she said. 'Tell me to butt out, but the engagement was so quick, so unexpected that even Tabby had no idea it was on the cards. The day before you announced it you were mourning your relationship with Octavia but went straight home to propose to someone else. Then there's the fact you are here...' She didn't say *kissing me*, but the words hung there between them. 'Something doesn't add up. I'm worried about you.'

As soon as she said the last words, she wanted to snatch them back. Who was she to worry about Charles St Clare Howard? But he didn't look angry or outraged at her presumption. Instead, he downed his pint, picked up his coat and stood up.

'Not here.' And with those cryptic words he strode towards the door. Liberty sat and stared after him for one long moment, then leaving her own pint unfinished, slipped on her own jacket and followed him. It was time for answers.

CHAPTER TEN

CHARLIE WAS TORN between betraying Millie's
confidence and the relief of unburdening himself. Usually when he was in any kind of trouble he would go to Millie or to Giles. But that
was out of the question. The recent phone call
showed that Giles was firmly team Millie right
now. And he didn't want his parents or Tabby to
know that he and Millie weren't a traditional romantic love match, for their marriage, or Millie
herself, to be diminished in their eyes.

And he owed Liberty an apology, one that
could only come with an explanation.

He set off down the small, narrow high street,
lined with a handful of shops to serve the community and the tourists, the usual small super-
market, butcher's, baker's and ironmongers
joined by gift shops and outdoor gear shops.
Liberty fell in beside him. It was dusk now, the
street lights on, lighting their way as they left

the village heading towards the huge iron gates which guarded the castle.

'I need to get married,' he said suddenly and abruptly. 'The title and estate are entailed, Tabby can't inherit, and we can debate the rights and wrongs of that forever, but right now that's a fact. The nearest heir is a second cousin twice removed who has no interest in the estate or farming or learning. So, I need to get married, and I really need a son.'

'You're a man, you don't have the same kind of biological clock women do. Why the hurry?'

'No, but I could get knocked over tomorrow,' he pointed out as they turned into the gates. The wide sweeping driveway was also lit up by just enough for them to find their way, the castle silhouetted in the distance. 'I could get ill. And if neither of those things happen and I put it off then I don't want to end up having to marry someone years younger.'

'But there are no guarantees. You could have trouble conceiving or be as fertile as the Nile but only have daughters. I can't believe I just said *only*, damn the patriarchy.'

'I agree. And if that happens then that's when we take a serious look at that pesky entail. But for now I owe it to my parents and the estate to at least try and do things traditionally. The problem is I have only been in love once in my life and I picked poorly.' He sighed. 'I say that I assumed that Octavia and I would settle down, that she would get bored of all the breaking up and making up and we'd head into a happy ever after, but in reality it was never going to happen. She thrives on drama, on being adored, on being part of society, she was never going to want to become a Norfolk farmer's wife and work in the family business.'

'No.' He could hear a quiver of amusement in Liberty's voice. 'She wasn't.'

'But I spent my whole adult life with her. I grew up with her. Learned about love with her.' He had no idea how to explain but he really wanted her to understand. 'What if that, I don't know, hardwired a template of what love *is*? Taught me that that is how a relationship works? What if I make the same mistake again? The future of the estate relies on stability.'

'The thing about mistakes, Charlie, is that we learn from them.'

'Ideally yes, but I can't risk getting it wrong again. The family business is too important to let emotion derail all we've built. I hadn't made any big decisions, but I had started to think the most sensible thing to do would be to look for someone I liked, who liked me, who understood my world, who didn't want to be swept off their feet but did want to settle down.'

'Then you and Millie realised you had feelings for each other, and you went straight to being engaged? I assumed you'd been secretly dating for some time, but this makes more sense. There seems to be so much you haven't discussed yet.' She inhaled. 'Not that it's any of my business.'

He stopped, turned to look down at her. 'Liberty, I need you to promise that you will never breathe a word of what I am about to say to anyone, especially not Tabitha.'

Her eyes widened. 'That sounds intense. I promise unless, you're not ill, are you? I can't keep that from Tabby.'

God, he was making a pig's ear of this. Was it even necessary? Liberty was making a good job of pretending the kiss had never happened, he should do the same. For her it had probably meant nothing. For him? No, better not to go there.

'No. I'm not ill. Look, I think you deserve some honesty from me, but some of this isn't mine to share which is why I don't want my parents or Tabby to know. The truth is that Millie…' He hesitated, trying to find the right words. 'She wants a big family, always has. And she would be—will be—a great mother. But time might not be on her side and if she wants to make sure she has that family she needs to get started pretty much straight away.'

'I see.'

'But she's not dated anyone for a long time, her ex screwed her over in a bad way and it has taken her some time to get over that. So there we are, neither of us is looking for romance, we both just want to be married and settled. We have the same goals. More importantly we love each other, respect each other, know each other better than ourselves in many ways...'

'But you're not *in* love with each other.' It was a statement not a question.

'Being in love is just about pheromones, chemicals. Something in your body reacts to something in someone else's body and that's it. It can lead you astray. But the end goal is to get to where Milly and I are now, we're just bypassing the messy, emotional phases. But I know my parents, her mum, Tabby, they'll be horrified, think of our marriage as less, not real in some ways. It's better for everyone that they think this is a whirlwind courtship between best friends. Do you understand?'

Liberty didn't reply, just resumed walking, her shoulders hunched against the wind, and Charlie had an urge to put his arm around her to shield her. Instead, he handed her his scarf and after a startled glance she took it, wrapping it around her neck.

By unspoken accord they headed round the side of the castle to the discreet door which led into the family apartment and into the boot room where they stayed silent as they hung their jackets up and took off their shoes before heading into the hallway. Usually, Charlie would head straight up to the turret study he had taken as his own, minimising alone time with Liberty, but he sensed their conversation wasn't yet done, so instead he followed her into the kitchen diner and accepted the large glass of red wine she handed him before she took a seat at the kitchen table, nursing her own glass. He leaned against the island, watching her intently.

Finally, she spoke. 'Do you think Mrs M would mind if I ate here instead of in the main house? I'm not sure I am up to seeing people. It's been a long day, week, month…'

'I'm sure she won't.' He hesitated. Should he offer to leave her alone to eat in peace? But he usually ate here, she knew that. 'After all, my dinner will be plated up.' It was an opportunity for Liberty to excuse herself, one she didn't take.

Less than ten minutes later their food arrived, Charlie meeting the housekeeper at the internal door to collect a tray, telling her to get herself home and promising to return the washed dishes to the main house before morning.

'When I speak to Mrs M I feel like I am a naughty twelve-year-old trying to scrump a pastry out of her kitchen,' he said when he returned and Liberty managed a tired smile.

'She adores and spoils you.'

'Oh, I know, this dinner is proof of that. Steak pie and mash. She's a queen, I should have married her, if only it wasn't for Mr McGregor.'

The joke hung there in the balance for a long few seconds before Liberty laughed, the flash of her dimple warming him through. 'Now marrying for food like this I do understand!'

'But you don't understand marrying for compatibility and similar goals?' She hadn't said so, hadn't said anything yet, but he sensed it.

Liberty didn't answer as she set the table, and he laid the food out, her expression thoughtful. 'What do I know?' she said in the end. 'I've never had a relationship last more than a few months, by choice, and I haven't exactly had shining examples of long-lasting marriage from my parents. Running after romance and true love has only brought my father a lot of alimony and my mother a nice collection of engagement rings. If this feels right to you then that's all that matters.'

Charlie was aware of a faint feeling of disappointment. What had he wanted her to say?

'It does,' he said firmly. Too firmly. As if he was trying to convince himself as much as her. 'But I have to admit I have needed some space to absorb it. We didn't expect the wedding to be quite so soon.'

'Hence you hiding up here while Giles and Millie face your family?'

He winced. 'Look, my ancestors might have excelled in battle, but I can promise every lance-wielding one of them would have been sent into a disorganised retreat at the sight of Tabby with a mood board.'

Liberty took another drink of her wine. Her cheeks had regained their colour, her eyes their usual intelligent gleam. 'So how will it work?'

'Like any other marriage. We'll respect each other, be faithful to each other...'

'That's a good thing. My father's second marriage was an open marriage, it did *not* end well.'

Charlie took a large sip of wine. 'Once we are married, that is.'

Her eyebrows drew together. '*What* is?'

'Being faithful. Everything has happened so quickly. I want Millie to be sure that this is what she wants, and like I say, she has been single for a long time. I don't want her to have any regrets. So, I made it clear that if she wants some romance while I'm away she should go for it. We've made no vows, no promises yet.'

Liberty put her fork down. 'Charlie Howard, are you saying that you and Millie have given *carte blanches* to each other to have some kind of last fling? Why are you telling me this? Why are you even here? Is *that* why you kissed me in the dome? Am I the lucky second choice *again*? Because we have been here once before and *you* broke my teenage heart.'

Why on earth had she said that? 'Teenage hearts are fragile, melodramatic things,' she said quickly, wanting to wipe the appalled self-loathing look off Charlie's face, to regain some dignity. 'Twenty-something hearts are much more resilient. Don't worry. I'm not in love with you. It was just one kiss and I feel a hell of a lot better knowing it wasn't completely wrong of us. I would have appreciated knowing that before though, I've felt pretty rotten over the last couple of weeks. I like Millie.'

Charlie looked discomfited, not an expression she was used to seeing on him. 'I know and I am so sorry. Look, yes, Millie said the exclusion applied to me too, but I hadn't planned to…' He shook his head. 'I'm not going to lie to you, Liberty. It was another really lovely kiss.' His voice dropped, almost to a whisper. 'Really lovely. But I had, *have*, no intent of using that exemption. I don't need to. Millie and I will have a good marriage, I'm convinced of that. And the best thing for me is enter it with no regrets or ties. But you were right, you deserved an explanation.'

'Thank you for the honesty.' Liberty looked down at her still half-full plate but her appetite was gone. Well, she'd asked for Charlie to be tell her what was going on and she had full disclosure. It wasn't Charlie's fault that she didn't like the answer. That no matter what he said, once again, she'd been Charlie's consolation prize. What an absolute fool she was.

She pushed her plate away and got to her feet. 'Of course, I will respect your and Millie's privacy. I won't breathe a word to Tabby and I genuinely hope you and Millie will be very happy. But I'm not willing to be a bit player in your love life a second time, Charlie.'

'I didn't…'

She held up a hand to silence him. 'It's obvious that we are attracted to each other, and under the circumstances that's a little less reprehensible than it seems. But that exemption of yours changes nothing. You don't want to use it and that's fine, but even if you did, I wouldn't be interested. I'm not a romantic, and I'm not a starry-eyed teen, but I do expect the men I sleep with to be mine for the duration at least. So, I think it's better not to spend too much time together from now on.'

She left the room quickly before Charlie could say anything else and made it to her bedroom before she felt tears press hot and hard. She blinked, forcing them back. She didn't cry, *especially* over men. It had been a kiss, that was all. She had known he was engaged. What did the circumstances of that engagement matter?

She opened her laptop and started to scroll through her emails, needing, wanting a knotty problem to absorb her, not wanting to figure out why she felt so raw, so hurt. Charlie hadn't been cheating on Millie, she hadn't been the other woman, her conscience was clear, she should be pleased. Relieved.

But she *was* the other woman. She wasn't the woman he was in love with, or the woman he wanted to make a life with. She was still the woman he kissed and left. Second best. Again. She bit her lip hard. What was wrong with her? Why did everyone walk away? Why did no one ever choose her?

This was why it was far better for her to set the rules. Easy, fun, time-limited relationships with no hard feelings when they came to their inevitable end.

But now she knew he wasn't in love with Millie, now she knew about their little pre-wedding clause she couldn't stop wondering what would have happened if they had stayed in the dome, if she had allowed him to back her onto that huge bed. What it would be like to touch him properly, for him to touch her. To make love to him?

The possibility of it hung in the air, tantalisingly close and possible. She could go downstairs right now and proposition him and for all his fine words about not intending to use the exemption she knew he would agree. In less than five minutes they could be naked, here in her bed, on the kitchen table, on the stairs...in all three places. Desire surged, hot and sweet and so tempting.

But no. She might be used to rejection, to being left behind, but she didn't need to search it out. She'd spent her adult life choosing her relationships carefully, making sure she was desired more than she desired, ending each one before her feelings came anywhere near to getting involved. And she was wise enough to know that Charlie Howard had always been her Achilles heel. That the only way to keep herself safe was to stay away. Far away.

And that was exactly what she going to do.

Liberty managed to keep her promise to herself as the shoot progressed. She didn't ignore

Charlie, that would have made it obvious to a cast and crew finely attuned to tension on a set that something had happened, but she was never alone with him. There were no more late-night drinks, no walks around the grounds, no more visits to the pub. She missed the easy friendship they had built up, and she spent more nights than she cared to admit, lying in bed and reliving every second of that kiss. How he had looked, what he had said, the feel of his hands on hers, the ragged sound of his breath. But then she would switch on her bedside lamp and read a chapter of her book until she had—almost—banished every illicit thought.

The end of the shoot couldn't come soon enough, she told herself. But at the same time she didn't want to leave. Didn't want to head back to the city, to her lonely flat. To a world where Charlie would be out of reach forever.

The days and weeks flew past, despite the long, sleepless nights, the temperature dropping week by week until there was no denying winter had finally arrived along with December, but Liberty was finding it hard to summon up any festive spirit. December meant the end of the shoot, the end of her time at Glenmere. And of course it was the month of Charlie's wedding, impossible to ignore thanks to Tabby's constant messages and an invitation she had yet to RSVP for, thanks to her own racing mind still dwelling on all he had told her in an unguarded minute. The only possible cure was to work even harder, to ensure she had no idle moments, no time to think, taking on any task she could, including organising the wrap party with Brad, the set designer, and Angus who clearly was as keen the shoot carry on as long as possible as she was.

'I can't believe there's just a week before you all pack up and go,' he said, when she walked into The Leaping Salmon to meet with him and Brad to finalise the last details. All the villagers and estate workers were also invited to the ceilidh in the village hall on the last day of the shoot.

Liberty leaned on the bar. 'You're not looking forward to getting rid of us?'

'Are you kidding? I'm praying every day for fiction to become reality and you all to be snowed in and have to stay another week.' He heaved a huge sigh. 'At least it's Christmas now and Charlie has managed to let the castle and most of the cottages for the whole festive season, so fingers crossed the guests all enjoy a dram or two at the atmospheric local pub.'

'Who could resist great food, a roaring fire and the best whisky selection in the Highlands? It's great that Charlie has managed to get the castle let.' She'd had no idea, not that she would

CHAPTER ELEVEN

WAS a good thing. The awkwardness
im and Liberty was intensifying with
ek and Charlie knew his sister would
n it the second they were all in the
m. The drive was a chance to clear the
urn to some kind of normalcy.
s, he and Liberty had both put their
the table. They were attracted to each
e, they were both youn~
ally unatt~~
ut neith
n. It wa
e wasn't
l into his
like the d
op that clu
ey scarf wraj
g out the colo
flush on her

expect to. Not while she avoided all conversation with him.

'How about you, Liberty? Looking forward to returning to London?'

'Not at all, I'm with you, if I could be snowed in here for the rest of the winter, I would be quite happy. And I have so much to do here and for home—Christmas is in just three weeks and I have done *nothing*. I still need to get presents for the cast and crew and decide what I am actually doing for Christmas although right now I am thinking sleeping is the perfect answer. Time has run away with me again.'

The not sleeping didn't help. Why hadn't she used those wide-awake times constructively and done some shopping rather than frittering them away on a series of crime novels she'd chosen for the total lack of any romantic subplot. The last thing she needed while she was getting over Charlie was to indulge in any romantic fiction. No, give her a high body count and a borderline alcoholic grumpy investigator instead.

Someone joined her at the bar. 'Why don't you take the rest of the day off and get some of your shopping done?'

Liberty turned to see Ted, the producer. 'Oh, I'm fine! Honestly! There's still plenty of time.'

'Liberty, you look exhausted. Besides, you haven't had a day off in months. We're nearly done, we can spare you for a day. Go, have a walk round, do your shopping, remind yourself there's a world outside this film.'

A world outside Glenmere. Maybe that was what she needed. 'You know, maybe I will. It's not even midday, I could be in Perth by early afternoon if I can just get a lift to the train station.'

Normally she would have hired a car but as Charlie had driven her up and she'd stayed firmly on-site she hadn't bothered.

Angus put down the glass he was polishing. 'Don't worry about a train. Charlie is heading to Perth, I'm sure he'll give you a lift.'

No no no. The last thing she needed was to be stuck in a car with Charlie for a couple of hours.

'It's fine, I don't want to put him to any inconvenience…oh, hi, Charlie.'

How had she not seen him? How had her Spidey sense not sent out an alert that he was in the vicinity? Why was he looking so unfairly good in his battered old jeans and cashmere jumper and tousled hair while she was looking like a location manager existing on three hours sleep a night at the end of a shoot with hair that needed a good washing and a hole in her own *not* cashmere jumper?

'Hi.' She tried to ignore the warm intimacy in the smile he directed her way. 'How are you, Liberty?'

'Good. Fine. F

'Liberty has so you say you wer Angus said cheer so palpable it was

Charlie's pause weren't looking ou it was there. Liber his every mood and

'Of course. Can y

'Yes, but I can eas

'That seems unne same way at the same park in thirty minute

And what could sh then.'

Half an hour to Pert She could manage that in Charlie's close prox launch herself at him. F

to smile as if she were anyone, greet her with a cheery. 'Ready?'

'As I'll ever be.'

'I feel that way about Christmas shopping too.'

'Is that what you are going in to do?'

'Christmas shopping and I just realised there are wedding gifts I need to bestow as well. If I had thought ahead I would never have agreed to getting married on Christmas Eve, it's doubled the amount of seasonal gift buying pain.' There, get the wedding mentioned and on the table straight away. No more secrets. Just a return to the old easy conversation.

'Are men really terrible at buying gifts or is it weaponised incompetence?' she asked sweetly and Charlie was shocked into laughter.

'Both,' he admitted. 'In my case anyway.'

'Christmas at least happens every year. It can't be that much of a shock.'

'True. But I usually buy Tabby whatever expensive item of clothing she sends me a link to, whisky for my dad, my mother gets whatever Tabby has chosen and wants me to go halves on, Aunt Flic new riding gloves or something like that. Only this year with the wedding Tabby has failed to send me any links or hints and so I am on my own. And that's the tricky part. According to Octavia I was absolutely useless although in my defence buying for her was a minefield. I set off more than a few explosions over the years.'

'What about Millie? What do you usually buy her?'

'Millie? Oh, Millie is easy, vouchers for a restaurant, tickets for a play or an exhibition, something like that. But this year we are spending Christmas as newlyweds with both our families. A voucher isn't going to cut it, is it?'

'No. Not nearly. And I guess for the wedding you need thank-you gifts, something for the bridesmaids and Giles, a thank-you for Tabby and both mothers.' She paused. 'A bridal gift for Millie.'

'That's it, all of the above. Basically, Christmas two days in a row. How about you, do you like buying presents?'

'I like the idea of it more than the reality I guess.' She looked down at her hands. 'The problem is not only do most of my siblings pretty much have everything, I don't know any of them well enough to buy something special, so it ends up being generic. Usually books.'

'You can't go wrong with books.'

'That's my motto.'

'You buy for all ten?'

'Yup. Not sure why, it's not always recipro-

cated and probably not appreciated, spot the one
only child in the whole dysfunctional family.'

'If you want to put your present buying skills
to good use you could always help me.'

'You want me to help you with your present
buying?' She sounded uncertain.

'I'll throw in dinner as a thank-you.'

Now why had he said that? Why hadn't he
made small talk about the landscape for half an
hour then left her at the car park with a cheery
see you back here at five?

Charlie knew why. It was because he had
missed her. Because this time together was hur-
tling towards its end, and he wasn't ready to say
goodbye yet.

Liberty stared out of the window, her body
language unreadable before she clearly came
to some kind of decision, her shoulders relax-
ing. 'Okay. But you can help me with mine in
return.'

The sky was overcast, the clouds low and
heavy and now they were so close to midwin-
ter it already felt like it was getting dark, which
made the cheerful lights of the pretty Christmas
market very welcome. The scent of hot chocolate, mulled wine and roasting chestnuts mingled in a festive cocktail as they browsed the
myriad stalls.

'I want to buy presents for the people I've

worked with the most and also for the director and cast,' Liberty explained. 'The producers will have something for us and for all the villagers who helped, but we usually exchange personal gifts too. I've learned to buy extras just in case someone I didn't expect surprises me with one.'

She murmured to herself as they perused the stalls. 'Whisky? Not all of them drink. Haggis bites? No use for the Americans on the crew, doubt they'll get them through Customs. Oh! Charlie, what about these?'

These were pretty little glass snow domes, a castle that looked remarkably like Glenmere in perched on a tree-lined mountain. 'Don't you just love snow globes?' Liberty picked one up and shook it, her eyes huge as she watched the snow whirl in the fantasy wintry landscape. 'I used to collect them as a child, but when Mum split up from Jack, well. My things weren't a priority.' She stopped, and for a moment the hurt blazed through, before she visibly fought it back. 'What do you think?'

'I think they are perfect.' Charlie found it hard to focus on the snow globes when Liberty was more dazzling by far, her hair like burnished fire, her eyes huge and luminous, filled with a mixture of nostalgia, sadness and excitement.

'Aren't they? This is brilliant, all sorted by the third stall! I'm going to go for it.'

Liberty arranged for the globes to be delivered to the castle and left the stall with a spring in her step. 'Okay. What's on your list? Shall we do Christmas first for both of us before we think about the wedding?'

The market and small independent shops that surrounded it were a treasure trove, and Liberty the perfect personal shopper. Her instincts and taste were unerring as she purchased locally made cashmere gloves for all her adult siblings, a gorgeous scarf for Tabby in a vibrant red they both knew his sister would love, a tweed hat for her father 'to wear for photo shoots on his country estate' and some locally made organic skincare for her mother.

'I am going to continue the tradition of buying books for all the children,' she said as they passed an inviting independent bookshop. 'They get whatever the must-have toys are times a million. There's no point buying them any, they just get lost.'

Charlie followed her example and guidance, purchasing locally made tweed cardigans for his mother, aunt and Millie's mother, the usual single malt for his father, a cashmere dress for Tabby and a carefully chosen selection of books for Millie, including some local cookbooks and one on the flora of Scotland he knew she'd like.

'And jewellery,' Liberty said as they dropped their bags back at the car. 'You should give her jewellery too. First Christmas and all.'

'Really? I'm going to get her something for the day before...'

'Then something matching,' Liberty said firmly. 'Come on, there's a couple of lovely jewellers along here.'

Left to his own devices Charlie would have been utterly clueless. There were several shops filled with bright and shiny rings, necklaces and other baubles, in every conceivable stone. It was quite frankly overwhelming. But Liberty was calm and focused, picking out gorgeous brooches, one a sprig of heather and one a thistle, for his mother and Millie's mother as a thank-you for hosting the wedding.

'I doubt your mother and Tabby have allowed Mrs Myles much say and she'll be too aware of her position to push in where she belongs but much more tactful to pretend you don't know this,' she said wryly. She also picked out pretty silver charm bracelets for Millie's two small cousins who would be her bridesmaids and a beautiful bangle for Tabby, a complicated twist of silver his sister would adore, while he selected some smart cuff-links for Giles.

'He does actually use cuff-links,' he said defensively when Liberty muttered something about an original choice and she laughed.

'He's a posh boy who works in the city. Of course he does.'

That just left Millie. Charlie was hard-pressed to remember what jewellery he had seen her wear. He wasn't even sure if her ears were pierced to Liberty's ill-hidden disgust.

'I know this isn't the most conventional of marriages but you have been friends with her for over twenty-five years! How can you not know if her ears are pierced?'

'They are because I remember them getting infected,' Charlie said triumphantly as Liberty whispered something that sounded very much like a repeat of her charge of *weaponised incompetence*.

'I'm just not observant about details that have very little to do with me,' he said with as much dignity as he could muster. But he did know that Liberty had pierced her ears several times, that she wore tiny delicate studs up her ears, and larger hoops at the front. That she often wore an amethyst pendant, a gift from her grandmother, and favoured a selection of chunky silver rings.

'What kind of engagement ring did she choose in the end?' Liberty asked and Charlie scrolled through his phone until he found the picture of the vintage emerald-and-ruby ring she had selected. Liberty took his phone off him and zoomed in, nodding approvingly.

'That's *gorgeous*. Okay, she likes character and history rather than new and bling, that makes sense, fits in with what I know of her. And rubies and emeralds, she's not afraid of colour. I don't think she's a pearl kind of girl even if it is her wedding day. Aha, how about this?' She'd stopped at an antique shop with an array of jewellery in the window and pointed at a matching set of ruby earrings and necklace in a dark gold setting dating from the nineteen twenties. 'You could give her say the earrings on your wedding day and save the necklace for Christmas? Or, how about the whole set for Christmas and that platinum bracelet for your wedding gift? That one there? It's got a similar vibe to the ring?'

On the surface it was all so normal, so easy. Two people who had known each other for much of their lives, who were working together, out shopping. They could discuss the wedding and Millie with no hint of diffidence, Liberty clearly taking her personal shopper role seriously. But underneath Charlie was aware of a deep undercurrent. The ever-strong pull of attraction, a sense of loss and a knowledge that he would want to hold onto this time. That he didn't want this day to be over.

Everything was purchased and safely stowed in Liberty's bag as they returned to the main market to reward themselves for their industry with a hot chocolate, Liberty insisting they head for the stall with the biggest queue and, not co-incidentally, the largest servings of lashings of whipped cream. The drink was indulgent and rich, warming him through. Charlie wished he could stop time, right here, just for a while.

'Oh look, Father Christmas!' Liberty came to an abrupt halt by an elaborate grotto, defined by a picket fence and covered in fake snow and some alarming looking reindeer automatons, the tinny sound of 'Rudolph the Red-Nosed Reindeer' blasting out on repeat. It was noisy and bright but she was completely absorbed as she watched the queue of small bundled-up children corralled by anxious parents as the excitement neared fever pitch. Two cold-looking elves hovered at the front of the queue.

'Look how excited they are. I envy kids at Christmas, all that anticipation and magic. I can't imagine having children of my own but if I did…' The wistfulness in her large grey eyes was painful to see. 'If I did then I want every Christmas tradition going. Reindeer food and pantomimes and even the elf on the shelf…'

'The *what*?'

'You've not heard of the elf on the shelf? It's a naughty elf who lives in your house over Advent and every night he gets up to another bit of mischief for the children to find when they get up the next day.'

'Why? What's wrong with an Advent calendar and a bit of chocolate every morning?'

'No idea why, but we will do it. And nativities and carols and a carrot for the reindeer.' Her voice trailed off and then she looked up at the sky and her whole face lit up. 'Oh, Charlie! It's snowing at last!'

Liberty loved snow, and she especially loved snow that fell thick and fast, dizzying flakes quickly blanketing the ground. When you added a Christmas market, fairy lights strung through trees, the very smell of Christmas in the air, well then it was just pure magic.

She turned slowly, head tilted up to the sky, eyes half closed. 'It's so beautiful.'

'Yes,' Charlie said hoarsely but when she looked at him, he wasn't looking at the sky, he was looking at her.

All around people were exclaiming, small children bending to pick up handfuls of the rapidly falling snow, the whole scene transforming into a winter wonderland before their eyes, but she barely took any of it in, her whole focus on Charlie. The last time she had stood in real snow with him, it had settled. They had been in the moonlit forest, taking part in a Hogmanay game of hide-and-seek, the world falling away, the voices of their friends fading in the distance. They had looked at each other just like this and then…

She had spent the last few weeks keeping her distance because she knew if she was alone with him then this would happen. That she would forget all the very many good reasons she should stay away and only remember how much she wanted him. How sure she was that he wanted her. That he was free for just a few short weeks, less. That it was now or never.

She really didn't want never.

Her breath hitched and before she knew what she was doing she took a step forward, her hands grasping his lapels as she looked steadily into his clear blue eyes.

'Liberty,' he said, half a whisper, half a prayer.

'I've been thinking about what you said.'

His mouth quirked into a half-smile. 'Which part?'

'All of it. I have no right to comment on your decisions. The kind of marriage you and Millie have chosen wouldn't work for me. If I was going to get married I would want all or nothing.' But then again, she was so scared of the *all* she opted for the *nothing*. After all, wasn't true love her parents' aim? And they didn't mind how many marriages it took to get there. How much damage they inflicted on those around. How could she ever be sure she got it right. Nothing was infinitely safer. 'But I get it. I do.'

'Thank you.'

'I've also been thinking about the other part, about the opportunity you gave Millie. I've been asking myself why you don't want it for yourself?'

His gaze didn't waver. She could see the heat in his eyes, knew he was holding onto his control by a thread. 'Because I knew the only woman I would want to sleep with was you, and I dragged you into my dramas once before. I swore never again, Liberty.'

'Very chivalrous. But do you know what would be the most gentlemanly thing to do?'

His raised eyebrows were a query.

'To let me decide for myself. I had a crush on you when I was twelve, Charles St Clare Howard, when you barely even registered my existence. I am too old and wise for crushes now, but I do still fancy you, and I don't want to spend the rest of my life wondering…'

'Wondering what?'

'Just how good we might have been.'

Charlie took her hands in his, his clasp tight. 'Liberty, I can't offer more than a few nights and you deserve more than that. But I have made a promise to Millie. I won't break that.'

'I know. I'm not asking you to.'

'I don't want you to get hurt.'

'I don't want to get hurt either. But I would like to enjoy a night, or two, or even a week of no strings sex with someone I find attractive and who finds me attractive. It's been a while.'

You don't let me in, her last boyfriend had complained, a sign it was time she ended it.

Well, here was someone who wouldn't want to be let in. Who would need all intimacy to be physical only. What could be more perfect?

Only the fact it was snowing and that the someone in question was Charlie.

'Charlie. I know you want me and you know I want you and we both know you are a free man right now. No one will get hurt but we could have a very nice time. But it's just a proposition. If you don't want to then let's go back to the car and I promise never to speak of it again.'

She did her best to sound like it was nothing to her. To make sure he didn't know how breathless she was as she waited for his reply.

'And if I do want to?' The words sounded dragged from him.

Her smile was slow. 'Snow is falling pretty

fast and you don't have your winter tyres on.
You should sort that, but I doubt any garage is
open now…'

She liked the light of mischief in his eyes.
'It is falling fast. It's probably not safe to drive
back tonight.' He'd swayed closer, his breath
warm on her cheek.

'Probably not. Guess we're stuck here for the
night. What shall we do?'

'What any two travellers stuck in a storm do?
Look for a friendly inn?'

'But what if they only have one room?'

His mouth curved into a wicked grin and her
insides melted. 'Now that I am counting on.'

Was she really doing this? Had she really
thrown caution and sense aside and proposi-
tioned Charlie despite several weeks telling herself how bad an idea it was?

Reality seemed blurred, dreamlike as she and
Charlie walked decorously side by side until
they found an anonymous if up-market chain
hotel and Charlie checked them in, with the easy
confidence and manner that defined him. Of
course they were upgraded to a suite, and of
course he suggested champagne, and actually
it was all so easy. A shower, a few emails to
say they had decided to make sure it was safe
to travel and so would head back in the morning. Champagne and a few mouthfuls of room

service, both wrapped in the huge hotel robes, light conversation, laughter, until it stilled, and the air became heated, charged, and she couldn't eat any more, drink any more.

With unspoken accord, they both stood at the same moment and then his mouth was on hers and he was loosening the belt of her robe as he backed her towards the bed, and it felt so right. She allowed herself to get lost in him, in the moment in a way Liberty had never been lost before. Kisses went from sweetly seductive to darkly intoxicating, she shivered at every touch, responding with an ardency and need that would have shocked her if she'd been able to form any coherent thoughts. His eyes blazed with passion as he held her gaze and she gloried in the way his breath quickened as she explored him, the gasps and sighs and moans. The rightness. There could be no regrets, no if onlys, they'd been granted this night and she was going to make the most of every second.

CHAPTER TWELVE

THE VILLAGE HALL was filled to capacity with villagers, cast and crew all whirling with various degrees of competency and knowledge to the local ceilidh band who had filled the space with their fast-paced music. Angus, smart in his kilt, microphone in his hand, stood next to them on the stage, clearly in his element as the caller.

Charlie bowed to his partner and stepped aside, realising he had ended up next to Liberty. It was as if there was a gravitational pull between them. No matter who he danced with, where he was, he was aware of her every step.

'Having fun?'

'So much. I love a ceilidh anyway and this band is brilliant. Isn't Angus a natural entertainer? He's wasted in a country pub.'

'He certainly made the most of the three lines you gave him in the film.' Charlie leaned against the wall and tried to focus on the dancers reforming into sets, not on Liberty, gorgeous in a green silk slip dress, her hair cascading down her back.

It had been a week since their trip to Perth. Any thoughts that their lovemaking was a one-night-only deal had been dispelled their first night back in the apartment. After all, what was the point of Liberty sleeping alone in one room and Charlie in another, missing each other, when they could just share a bed? And, as Liberty said, it made sense for them to make sure they had really got each other out of their system before Christmas Eve. It had been a suggestion Charlie had only been too happy to oblige.

But the problem was he was by no means sure he was anywhere near getting Liberty Gray out of his mind or his thoughts or any system at all. The opposite in fact. The more he touched her, the more he wanted her. Just standing next to her, watching the dancers, he couldn't believe that no one knew about them; he felt as if there was a neon sign over their heads, that the pull between them was visible. But Angus, and Ryan, the actor playing the lead, and the main cameraman kept flirting with Liberty and he kept fielding off questions about his very much impending nuptials which meant the pair of them were pretty good actors indeed.

Angus called a Duke of Perth and the sets reshuffled as couples took their places. The village and film cast and crew were intermingled, the villagers patiently helping coach the film folk through the steps, although some had a more natural affinity than others. Liberty and Charlie both knew most of the dances and had joined the villagers in taking on the newbies, changing partners each time.

Charlie held out a hand to Liberty. 'Dance with me?'

She flushed. 'Should we?'

'It would look more suspicious if we didn't. Besides, it's a ceilidh not a waltz. More's the pity.'

'You fancy that, do you? A candle-lit ballroom, you in skintight breeches and a cravat, leading your lady into a scandalous dance.'

'Depends on the lady.'

Liberty took his hand and allowed him to lead her onto the floor to join three other couples in search of a fourth. She leaned in just before they were within hearing distance. 'Maybe we can role-play later.'

'I'll dig out my breeches.'

'Promises, promises.'

Charlie followed the instructions almost mechanically. On the surface he was laughing, exchanging breathless comments with their set partners, listening to Angus as they went through the intricate steps. He loved ceilidhs, the fun, the exertion, the music, the way everyone could join in whether they had learned the steps at school or were trying for the first time. But right now, he would prefer a darkened dance floor and hidden corners he could whisk Liberty into.

The film crew had packed up. Tomorrow they would all be gone. He didn't know when Liberty was planning to leave but he could see no reason for her to stay much longer.

Which meant there was no reason for him to stay. A general manager had been appointed and had already moved into the rooms set aside for her, the events manager was starting after Christmas. Mrs McGregor had the staff she needed to get the castle and cottages ready for the festive season, full-time bar staff and waiting staff had been employed and a new chef was expected the next day.

Glenmere Castle was launched. His job was done. Only one vase had been broken over the last two months, the insurers were happy, the accountants were happy. He could walk away knowing he had done a good job.

Back to normality. Normality with a twist. Because in less than two weeks' time he would be married.

And once they left Scotland he and Liberty would be over.

The reel came to an end and the dancers whooped their approval as Angus announced a break. Charlie scooped two glasses of wine and handed one to Liberty.

'I could do with some air,' he said.

'Me too.'

They weren't the only ones. The porch and car park were filled with hot revellers taking the opportunity to cool down, even though the temperature was below freezing and snow still covered the ground. 'I can't believe this is the last night,' Liberty said. 'It's been a great shoot. I've loved working with them all. That's the problem with freelancing, you get into a rhythm and then onto the next.'

'Do you have another job lined up?'

'In January. I think I might take a few weeks off, properly off I mean, go away. I don't have Christmas plans so some sunshine sounds in order. I just need to book something.'

'You're not coming to Howard Hall for Christmas.'

'With the wedding the last thing any of you need is extra people for Christmas and besides, it all feels too soon. I want us to be friends, Charlie. I don't have many close friends for one reason or another, and Tabby is like a sister to me. I would hate what has happened to ruin that, for us to be awkward with each other, but time is probably a good thing. We will need to readjust and you need to concentrate on Millie.'

She was right. 'Are you heading back tomorrow? I should know this,' he added.

Her smile was pure wickedness. 'Not necessarily, we haven't done much talking recently. No, I need to go through the house with Mrs M and make sure we have stuck to the contract, check any damage, help put everything back to how it was etc., so I'm planning on staying on for about a week. Which is a good thing because I really need to fix my flight back. I am usually much more organised than this!'

'I am planning to stay on for a bit as well.' Charlie had planned for just a couple of days, but now he thought about it a week made sense. Professionally and personally. 'I want to meet the chef tomorrow, help them settle in and make sure Mrs M and the newer staff have all they need for Christmas. In fact, why don't I drive you back?'

'You don't need to do that, Charlie.'

'I want to. Full circle.'

'Okay. But if you change your mind…'

'I'll make sure you get on a plane. But I won't.'

Charlie wasn't lying, he did want to meet the chef again and show him around; the general manager was new in post and Mrs McGregor had more than enough to do without settling in new staff, but he also knew that arriving home less than a week before the wedding would raise some eyebrows.

Let them be raised.

'Come on,' he said. 'I think they're starting up again. Another?'

'Absolutely but I am afraid I am promised to another.' Her voice dropped. 'But that's okay, we can dance later. You promised me a waltz, I believe.'

Their gazes caught, held and for one long moment everything fell away but her. What would have happened, be happening if things were different? If Millie hadn't accompanied him to the wedding? If there was no engagement, no fast-approaching wedding of his own? Instead of wringing every second out of this too short-term fling would they be looking into the future? Making plans to meet in London, to keep their liaison secret over Christmas so Tabby didn't guess because it would still be such early days?

Or was Liberty here because he wasn't free? Because this could only be short and sweet then over. Tabby often bemoaned her friend's self-fulfilling prophecy when it came to relationships.

'She thinks they won't work out so they don't work out,' she had said. 'Either she picks the absolute worst, or, if she allows anyone vaguely decent in then she bins them before they get too close. Rejects before she gets rejected. It's infuriating. I wouldn't mind if she was happy.'

Charlie didn't think he was the absolute worst, he hoped not anyway, but he could see how the time limit imposed on their relationship made him safe. Made her safe. And who could say that if he was free that things would work out between them? He had allowed love and passion to dominate his teens and twenties and it had been a complete disaster. He wasn't marrying Millie just because they both wanted children and because time wasn't on her side but because she offered him safety from that, a sanctuary. With Millie he was guaranteed not to make the same mistakes again. Whereas Liberty had plenty of demons of her own, demons he wasn't sure she even *wanted* to conquer. Any relationship with her was bound to hit obstacles, to naturally have the kind of drama and emotional baggage he had sworn to avoid.

He had made Millie a promise. He couldn't let her down. Especially not when the alternative was so uncertain.

No, it was better this way, but as he followed Liberty back into the overheated hall he wished it wasn't. That he could take her hand in front of everyone, whirl her into the dance, into the future; instead it was a few more furtive nights and a goodbye.

Just over two months ago there had been a real danger this film wouldn't happen, and now it was all over. Most of the cast and crew were gone, just a handful left to return Glenmere Castle to its restored glory.

It was a different place to the one she had driven to in the autumn. There were more staff, the whole estate filled with purpose as they prepared for the lucrative Christmas season. Everywhere Liberty walked she could see activity, windows washed, pathways cleared, Christmas decorations put up, lights strung through trees. The general manager had finally moved into her apartment, the chef had arrived and was making the kitchen his own. There was an air of new adventures, a new era. And it didn't include her. Her time here was done, her time with Charlie was done.

Liberty looked around. She had walked with no destination in mind, trying to clear her head, and yet it was no surprise that she had ended up here, where it had all begun nearly eight years ago. A snow-covered glade, the weak wintry sun peeping through the pines on the nearby slopes, bare trees, their spindly branches heavy with snow. It had been that oak there. Her back against it, glad of the support because her knees refused to hold her up, her whole body on fire, aching, wanting. It was more than she had ever felt, imagined, and so very right. It was every book; he was every hero and she was playing the central role for the first time in her life. Dreams did come true. Charlie Howard had not just noticed her, but he wanted her too.

Her mind had flashed forward, Charlie visiting her at university, walking hand in hand by the river, Christmases like this where she wasn't just Tabby's poor friend, *it's very sad you know, lovely girl but she has nowhere to go. Her parents, well...* no, she would be part of the family.

And then he had unzipped her jacket, and his hands were under her top and his mouth was so hungry and demanding and yet so sweet she wanted to be absorbed into him. She was so glad she had waited, hadn't succumbed to the pleas of her handful of school and university boyfriends. She must have known that this moment awaited her.

But then footsteps, a laugh, a well-bred drawl. And five minutes later she was alone, her jacket still undone, lips still swollen...

She inhaled shakily, horrified to find tears brimming in her eyes. She was glad of that night, glad of the lessons it had taught her, the walls it had helped her erect around her heart, the way the memory kept her safe. Even now.

She had to hold onto that, remember to keep herself safe. After all, no one else would.

She had said at the ceilidh that she didn't want things to change. That she needed his friendship. But she had been fooling herself. She needed a lot more than that and she could never have it.

It was ironic, she'd spent her life indulging in short-term relationships, she'd thought she was well equipped to handle this. That she would be able to walk away untouched. She should have known better.

The only question now was how she disentangled herself with her pride intact.

'Hey, I've been looking for you.'

Of course Charlie had found her. She blinked again, forcing a smile onto her face as she turned to face him. God, he was everything she wanted him to be. Still that storybook hero of her teenage dreams. But a hero with feet of clay.

'Back to where it all began.'

He closed his eyes briefly, regret and pain flitting across his face. 'I am so sorry…'

'No.' She shook her head. 'We've been over this. There is no need.' Once she would have lapped up his apology, wanted the validation it gave her, but no more. Her heart gave a painful jolt at the sight of him, hair falling over his face, tall, eyes creased in concern, hoping she was okay. Charlie Howard always wanted everyone to be okay. He was the perfect brother, son, employer and friend. Look at him riding to Millie's rescue with no thought of the consequences. It was what he did. That was why he'd been the perfect boyfriend for a messed-up party girl, thinking he could save Octavia although the last thing she wanted was to be saved.

The one person he had never tried to save was her. She wasn't going to let him start now.

'You know,' she said. 'There's a tree over there that holds rather good memories for me.' She ignored the fact that some of her darkest memories were also associated with this spot. 'Want to make some more?' She held his gaze as she walked slowly to the tree, leaning against it provocatively.

'There's a warm, comfortable bed just ten minutes' walk away.'

'Just a kiss, Charlie, then we can discuss that bed.'

He held her gaze, his own smouldering, and her body responded the way it always did, immediately hungry for him. She leaned back further, tilting her head towards him. This would look a lot more seductive in a dress rather than leggings and a puffer jacket, but the look on

Charlie's face showed that the clothes were no barrier to his imagination.

He finally reached her and put one hand on the tree by her head, leaning in until their faces were just millimetres apart, still holding her gaze. The intent mixed with the space between them was dangerously seductive, and Liberty's breath started to speed up in line with her pulse. It was dangerous how addictive he was.

'Are you just going to look at me or are you planning to kiss me any time soon?' She had meant to sound seductive but to her horror the words hitched in her throat, came out more as a plea than a challenge. His eyes darkened to navy, his mouth an irresistible curve.

'Oh I am planning to kiss you all right.'

Her knees weakened so much that if she hadn't had the tree for support, she was sure she would have staggered.

'Promises, promises.'

How could eyes say so much? Want and desire and need mingled with appreciation and humour—and regret. They both knew this was near its end. But only Liberty knew when. She wasn't prepared to have her life decided by someone else's timetable. Being the one to walk away was the only power she had.

'Patience,' he murmured, but Liberty was setting the rules. She cupped his cheek and leaned right back into him, folding her body into his, satisfaction filling her as he groaned. Leg against leg, hip against hip, her body as moulded to his as the layers allowed, she snaked an arm around his neck so she could angle him just where she wanted him.

'I'm done with patience.'

She felt his rumble of amusement reverberate through her, the shift in her balance as he took back control, pushing her back against the tree and now he was cupping her face as he finally, finally kissed her. Tantalisingly sweet, tantalisingly slow, a gradual increasing pressure. She was boneless, surrendering to him. *His.* The thought hung there, shocking and stark until she pushed it away, not wanting anything to mar the moment. Instead she unzipped his jacket, slipping her hands under his shirt, tugging at buttons, wanting to feel and be felt despite the snow all around. There was no more talk of beds or moving, Charlie responding to the change in pace, the urgency in kind.

Time stopped. There was only this. The kiss, that ratcheted up from sensual and teasing to urgent in seconds, hands exploring, kisses hard and hot, her hands working at his jeans, his hand inside her leggings as she impatiently slid them down. This is what she had wanted eight years ago, her inexperienced heart and body leading her towards this claiming, but who was claiming who she still didn't know. The tree was rough against her back and head, the air cold on exposed skin, the angle awkward, but she didn't care as he pressed closer, harder, his touch everywhere she needed it to be, his clever fingers making her gasp out loud, and cling to him, her own hands digging into his shoulders, her leg wrapping around him as he finally entered her. She buried her face in his neck, kissing, nipping, gasping, both glorying in the moment and mourning the moment they would both be spent.

Liberty had no idea how long they were there, but she gradually returned to herself, Charlie heavy against her. Slowly, without words, they disentangled themselves, redoing buttons and zips with cold hands.

'You were right,' Charlie said, pulling her close. 'We didn't need a bed. But you must be freezing, why don't we go warm up? I have some ideas on how we can do that...'

It was tempting, so very tempting. Liberty allowed herself to touch his cheek, to run a finger along his cheekbone and across his mouth before standing on tiptoes for one last lingering kiss. 'That sounds amazing but I need a quick shower. My lift leaves in half an hour.'

'Your what?'

'To the airport. I'm getting a lift with Bill.'

'But…' His eyebrows drew together. 'I thought you were coming back with me tomorrow. What's the hurry?'

'I think it's better we have a clean break, don't you?' Slowly, almost painfully, she disentangled herself, standing back, immediately cold, the inches between them a chasm.

'Yes, but why now when we still could have tonight?' His gaze sharpened. 'What's going on, Liberty?'

'Nothing.' She started walking back to the castle and after a second's hesitation he fell in beside her. 'I just have a chance to get back today and took it. No big deal.' She inhaled. It was time to take that control she had promised herself. 'Look, Charlie, the rules were clear from the start. We were here to have some fun. We've done that. What we did just now ticked off a little teenage fantasy of mine, it feels like the perfect way to finish, full circle, don't you agree?' She sounded as unconcerned as she could. As if the words, the sex, him, meant nothing.

'If that's what you want then of course.' Typical Charlie, always the gentleman. 'But I still don't get why so sudden. Is there something more going on?'

'You'd like that, wouldn't you?' She hadn't meant to say that but she couldn't stop herself. 'Then you could try and fix me.'

'What are you talking about?'

'You genuinely don't see that I am quite happy with how things are. To you I am poor, damaged Liberty, another entry on your roster of ladies in distress.'

'What?' Shock reverberated through his voice.

'Come on, Charlie. You thrive on riding to the rescue, the more doomed the better. You should have lived a thousand years ago and had some nice dragons to slay.'

'I have no idea what you're talking about.'

'No? Tell me, Charlie, did you never dream of another life? A city career like Giles, surrounded by your tribe as you make money. A tech startup, an office filled with boy toys and a real ale bar on Fridays? Acting, travelling, politics, anything?'

'No. Never.' The words were curt. He was getting angry. Good. She needed that anger, it made everything easier.

'No, because you had to take over the family business, nobly and selflessly. The perfect son and heir, the perfect brother, the perfect boyfriend, loyal to your lady no matter how undeserving. Anyone with half a brain could see Octavia didn't want or need saving, but how much more romantic the narrative if she did. You even let her win in the end, like a true knight would. Now you have ridden to Millie's rescue, but before that you couldn't help but detour to me. Trying to assuage your guilt over one kiss years ago that meant nothing. God, Charlie, do you really think my heart was broken back then? That I was so weak? I just told you what I knew you wanted to hear.'

It felt good, to say the bitter words, to see the anger growing on his face. Good, and yet at the same time they tore her apart.

His face was set into hard lines. 'Do you think I don't know what's going on here?'

'I'm sure you think you do.'

'Liberty Gray pushing me away, just as she pushes everyone. So scared of getting hurt, she would rather sabotage first.'

Good point and well made. It was a tactic that had kept her safe over the years. She just normally wasn't this obvious—or cruel. But these weren't normal circumstances. She didn't normally feel this vulnerable, this needy. She didn't normally wonder if her heart was actually engaged this time, and that's why it felt like it might just be cracking, fault lines running through it widening and shattering.

'Maybe I am, maybe I am just being honest.

We both knew the rules, Charlie, so let's not make this something it's not. You have a wedding to go to. I hope you'll both be very happy.'

Charlie stopped, his hands in his pockets, his face a mixture of incredulity, anger, sorrow and a pity that tore at her and enraged her in equal measure. 'I'm not doing this, Liberty,' he said. 'Look. Let's go back to the apartment, talk properly there.'

'There's nothing more to say. Besides, my plane ticket is booked.'

'Okay then. If this is really what you want. But, Liberty. Stop pushing people away, they might just surprise you. And I am sorry, I didn't mean to hurt you.'

Her smile was as careless as she could make it. 'You didn't.'

'That's good.' She hated the disbelief in his voice.

He turned and started to walk away from the castle, towards the loch, head held high. She should have kept walking, but she couldn't move, had to watch him walk out of her life for good. He hadn't made it ten paces before he stopped and turned to look at her. 'Do you think I'm making a mistake?'

Of all the questions at all the times. 'It doesn't matter what I think, Charlie. You'll do what you think is right. Just like you always do.' And then she did walk away, knowing she was leaving part of her heart behind her.

CHAPTER THIRTEEN

IT WAS THE day before Christmas Eve. The day before his wedding and Charlie felt completely numb. He just needed to see Millie, to remind himself of all the reasons this marriage with guaranteed calm and happiness was the right thing to do. He'd hoped to see her before now, but he had been flat out catching up with all the hands-on work he hadn't been able to do whilst in Scotland, and Millie herself seemed too busy to come to him or to do more than exchange a few quick messages. Giles had been equally elusive.

He'd deliberated calling Liberty, but in the end hadn't even messaged. She'd made her feelings very clear and he had to respect that. Besides, he would only be calling to assuage his own conscience.

He'd known getting involved with her was a bad idea. He'd never had a no strings feelings-free fling in his life. Sex to Charlie meant something. He'd been kidding himself when he'd thought he could walk away unscathed. And here he was, on the eve of his wedding, thinking about another woman.

'Here you are! I've been looking for you everywhere. What are you doing on the roof?' Tabby. He'd been avoiding her, sure she would see the guilt in his eyes.

'Getting some air, thinking.'

His sister came and joined him. 'Remember when we were absolutely forbidden to come up here?'

'I'm not sure that ban was ever lifted.' Accessible from an attic window, the flat area, flanked by two vast chimney-stacks, had been an irresistible draw at every age. 'I love how you can see almost the whole estate from here, the sea and the horizon. Tabs?'

'Hmm?'

'Do you think I have a saviour complex?'

'Do I think you have a *what*?' She slanted a keen look at him. 'Is this about Octavia? Because a, that was a mug complex if anything and b, tomorrow you are marrying a wonderful woman who we all love and Octavia should be at the very end of a long list of things on your mind.'

'She is! Don't worry. There won't be three of us in this marriage.' At least, he didn't want there to be, but it wasn't Octavia's icy elegance that haunted his dreams but Liberty's burnished gold vibrancy. 'No, it was something Liberty said.' Just saying her name felt dangerous. 'Like, I never considered another career, I did exactly what was expected of me…'

'And that's a problem because? Look at what you inherit, Charlie.' She waved her arm dramatically. 'And you love it, you know you do.'

He exhaled. 'I do, it's just…and yes, Octavia. All those years I put up with her drama and all the rest because I thought I was the only one who could…' He grimaced. 'You're right, I was a mug.'

'Charlie, are you getting cold feet? Because Mum and I have put a lot of work into this wedding. But your happiness is more important, obviously,' she finished more than a little doubtfully.

'No.' He meant it. He'd given his word and this marriage made sense, he just needed to remind himself why. 'I just need to see Millie, that's all.'

'You're in luck. That's her car there just turning up the drive? Giles's car anyway, he's giving her a lift. Come on, stop philosophising on the roof and come and see your bride.'

It was a good plan, and Charlie was desperate to see Millie. But as they edged their way back to the large open attic window he couldn't help but ask. 'Have you heard from Liberty since she got back to London?'

'Not much. I've been so busy with all the last-minute wedding plans and she usually needs some decompression time after a shoot. I was hoping she would come for Christmas Day even though she couldn't make the wedding...' Liberty had been invited to the wedding? She had never said. 'But she says she is heading off somewhere. She was looking for a last-minute flight.'

'Good, that's good.' How could he have made his vows knowing she was listening, watching, that she knew the truth?

And then he was on the stairs and Millie was walking in, looking a little diffident, nervous, but her own glorious, welcoming, safe self and he was hugging her.

'Everything okay?' There was a hint of strain around her eyes.

'It's all going to be fine now,' she said, leaning in tight. Charlie's conscience smote him. He'd left her to do everything. While he was off adjusting and forgetting and dallying she had been organising and planning. He didn't deserve her. But he was going to make her happy, just as they had planned. No matter what it took.

* * *

Vow made, Charlie just wanted to get on and get married already. But there was a timetable to follow, starting with a rehearsal in the family chapel. He felt more like an actor than a groom as he stood in the small, sacred space, practising his lines, Giles looking unusually solemn next to him. Once that was done his duties continued with a formal rehearsal dinner in the dining room. Charlie knew exactly what was expected of him as host and heir on these occasions and so he made polite small talk before officially welcoming the guests who were staying overnight to Howard Hall and his wedding, complimenting Millie with a few lines that made her blush. It wasn't hard, she looked sensational in a green silk dress.

But he still wasn't attracted to her.

He was very proud of her though. She wasn't used to these occasions but her nerves didn't show as she made her own speech at the end of the meal, an elegant and heartfelt thanks to everyone who had helped.

'Finally,' she said. 'I want to say a special thank-you to Charlie's best friend and best man, Giles. When Charlie's work dragged him away, Giles stepped up and helped me organise all sorts of wedding-related things—from invitations to flowers and rings. And I can tell you, he can now put together a pretty impressive festive wreath, too! Seriously, though. Thank you, Giles, for everything.'

Millie looked across at Giles as she said this and he looked steadily back and for one moment his heart was in his eyes. Charlie sat there frozen. *Giles was in love with Millie?* Surely not. Attracted to, yes, but in love? He *had* been very protective of her. And wreath-making? That didn't fall into best man duties.

Besides, that look…it was unmistakable.

His best friend in love with his bride. Was she in love with him too?

Sleep was always going to be difficult but the revelation at the dinner made it impossible. He needed air and he needed a drink. Charlie grabbed a bottle of champagne and despite the temperature, headed outside to the ruined folly that had once been Millie's and his hideout.

He sat on the wall and took a swig from the opened bottle, thinking over what he had seen. *Was* Millie in love with Giles? If so, what did that mean. Giles was so adamantly anti marriage or commitment and a family, and those things were so important to Millie.

But how could she marry him if she was in love with someone else? Neither of them had planned for that contingency. Although as far as Millie was concerned, he still had feelings for Octavia. No wonder, he had allowed her to think that.

And yet it was so far from the truth it was laughable. He had barely thought about Octavia in months.

If he was in love with anyone, it was Liberty. Love. Liberty.

Was this love? How was he expected to know when he had got it so very wrong before? He did want to protect her, help her, not because of some saviour complex but because he cared, because her happiness mattered to him. He desired her, enjoyed her company, loved to see her at work, hair tucked behind her ears, nose screwed in concentration. Liked her humour. Her directness. She'd made her feelings very plain, but Charlie knew her well enough to suspect that she had been masking. Pushing him away so she was the one to leave. Knew how vulnerable she was to rejection.

He heard footsteps and looked up to see a small figure walking towards him, wrapped in a big coat over pyjamas and wellies at least a size too large. 'Millie?'

'Who else? Did you bring a second glass for me?' She joined him on the wall.

'I didn't even bring one for me.' He handed the bottle to her. 'I wasn't really expecting company.'

'Why not? We always used to meet here as kids. And teens, for that matter.'

'Yeah, but…everything's different now, isn't it?' And that was the last thing he wanted.

'I suppose. But if we're really getting married tomorrow, I don't *want* it to be different. I want it to be like it always was between us. Don't you?'

And there it was. '*If* we're getting married? Having doubts?'

'No,' she countered. 'Why, are you?'

Was he? She was Millie. He loved her. All his reasons for marrying her were unchanged. Whereas Liberty…he wanted her, desired her, but she unsettled him. And the way things had ended were reminiscent of Octavia at her worst. He had a good thing here; he shouldn't sabotage it. And hurting Millie was unthinkable. If she really wanted to go ahead then there was no other path. 'Of course not.'

She leaned against him and neither spoke for a while, Charlie's mind whirling. The look in Liberty's eyes as she deliberately set out to hurt him. She hadn't looked bored or amused or contemptuous, she had been defensive. The look in Giles's eyes when Millie made her toast. The rawness, he had never seen Giles like that before. He couldn't just ignore it.

'So… Giles. He really was a help? I know

you two haven't always got on so well, and I really did feel bad about having to go away and leave it all to you two, but—' Smooth, Charlie. Very smooth.

'No. He was great. He… I couldn't have done it all without him.'

'Good.' He could leave it, maybe he should. But at the same time… 'Only…the way he was watching you at the dinner. I wondered if… maybe something had happened between you two?'

Millie let out a groan. 'Were we that obvious?'

'You weren't but he was. To me, anyway.'

'I'm sorry.' She sounded mortified. 'We didn't mean for it to happen. It was just—'

'It's fine.' The last thing he deserved was an apology. 'We both agreed that if we wanted to have a last few weeks of freedom, we should. And at least it was Giles. I don't have to worry about his stealing you away and marrying you before I can.' It was a shame Giles was so opposed to marriage; the irony was that he would make a great husband, kind and conscientious underneath that charming exterior. But if even Millie couldn't change his mind, then his friend really was set on living life alone. And that meant Charlie's promise to Millie stood. He couldn't let her down, not if she wanted to go ahead.

'Right. What about you? Did you find someone to...sow those last wild oats with in Scotland, while you were away?' He shifted uncomfortably. 'You did! Who was she?'

She'd been honest with him, he needed to be in turn. There was no point starting marriage with a lie. 'You should know I didn't intend to, but I think there was always unfinished business between Liberty and me. I made it very clear I was committed to you, and she made it very clear she wasn't interested in anything serious, and like I said, unfinished business. But it's done, now,' he said as earnestly as he could, meaning every word. It *was* done, and whatever he felt about that, about Liberty, had to be locked away and never thought of again. 'And I'm here. I'm committed to you, Mills. I won't let you down, I promise.'

'I know.' She took the bottle from him and held it up. 'To us.'

'To us.' And he meant it. At least, he really wanted to mean it. And that was a good start.

Liberty stared at the clothes tossed on her bed. Thermals and jumpers and all the things she had taken to Scotland on one side, bikinis, flip-flops and little dresses on the other, a now empty suitcase between them. Her flight was booked. Like the heroine in *Jingle Bell Highlander*, she was avoiding Christmas by taking off. By the time she landed in Thailand it would be Boxing Day. She fully intended to lose track of time in an orgy of sunbathing, sleeping and reading.

She just had to get through the rest of Christmas Eve. She had hoped to sleep through it but no such luck. It had been a fitful night and she had ended up getting up before six to search out coffee from the early-opening café down the road, throwing a coat over her pyjamas so she could take it straight back to bed.

She wasn't a fan of Christmas Eve at the best of times. Christmas Eve as Charlie's wedding day felt infinitely worse. A reminder in every way of just how lonely she was.

Thanks to Tabby she knew every carefully timetabled moment from the wedding rehearsal yesterday followed by a formal meal, to the pre-wedding drinks and the timing of the service itself. Roll on the moment it would all be over, and she would be free.

Only free to *what*? Work as much as possible so she didn't get the opportunity to feel? Free to look for relationships that had *short-term* tattooed all over them? Free to keep her heart locked away? It was existence, not really freedom.

What would have happened if she had played it differently? If she had told Charlie she was falling for him? Had fallen for him. That the crush which had never quite gone away had crystallized into something real. If she had been honest when he asked her what he should do? She felt flayed at the thought of making herself so vulnerable, putting herself up for rejection. But without vulnerability how could she ever move on, have a fulfilling life, a proper relationship, a family?

She had been so scathing of Charlie's white knight tendencies but she still had wanted him to fight for her, for them. She was still poised for the bell to ring, to see him there at her front door, in his wedding suit, to tell her it had been her all along. To tell her he understood why she had pushed him away. That he loved her. That it had always been her.

Liberty sat on the bed and took a deep breath, pushing back the threatened tears. She hadn't cried over Charlie Howard for eight years, she wasn't going to start now. Instead, she was going to force herself back into the real world, pack her bag and then find a way to occupy herself until her flight finally took off in just under twenty-four hours' time.

She still had her mother's present to wrap and give along with her half-siblings and stepfather's gifts. She'd sent her presents to everyone on her father's side from Scotland, with no expectation of seeing any of them over the festive period, but she usually tried to hand her mother's over in person. She could take a trip out to the Edwardian house backing onto Richmond Park. There would be a scrupulous timetable of festive activities of course, but surely there would be a thirty-minute slot available she could fit in to? The journey to and from Richmond would nicely fill several hours.

Not that her mother had asked if she was planning to visit or suggested that she did but if Liberty waited for an invitation, she would never see her.

Liberty retrieved the tote bag filled with the still unwrapped presents that Charlie had helped her choose. The books for her siblings. *The Dark is Rising* quintet for the oldest, a selection of Diana Wynne Jones for the next and several illustrated books of myths for the youngest. The carefully chosen organic skincare for her mother. The history books for her stepfather. And a wrapped parcel. What was this? She hadn't put it there. She eased it out. It was a box, wrapped in red paper.

'What on earth?' She couldn't see a tag, but there was a scrap of Sellotape as if one had been attached at some point, and sure enough, when she shook the bag out, a glitter-covered cardboard rectangle fell onto the bed.

Dear Liberty. Time to restart the collection? Happy Christmas. All my love, Charlie xxx

All my love. It was the kind of thing people wrote all the time, it didn't mean anything.

But he had bought her a gift and hidden it. Surely that did.

With slightly shaking hands she undid the Sellotape and carefully peeled the paper back, revealing a cardboard box. She opened it up and there, nestled on strips of paper packed in tight to keep them safe, were three snow globes of differing sizes. The smallest was the same as the ones she had handed out as gifts, the wintry scene resembling Glenmere, the second a Victorian London scene, the largest a fantasy of mountains and trees, a sleigh flying through the air. She swallowed, remembering the brief conversation in Perth. *I used to collect them as a child*, she had said, and then stopped. Tried to hide her hurt at her mother's casual attitude to her belongings, but Charlie had seen. He had seen her.

She put the box down, her mind whirling, her heart speeding up, her emotions a kaleidoscope. She loved Charlie, there was no point pretending otherwise, and if there was any chance he felt the same way then she had to tell him, preferably before the wedding which was in… oh, God, it was in five hours. She was still not dressed, in London and she had to get to Norfolk on one of the busiest travel days of the year.

Charlie Howard might not be charging in on his white horse to save her but that was fine. She was a modern woman. She could save him instead. As soon as she was dressed and could figure out how to get there, that was.

CHAPTER FOURTEEN

CHARLIE HAD BARELY drunk at the rehearsal dinner, and they hadn't finished the champagne, so why did he feel in the grips of the worst hangover ever? He couldn't stop his hands from shaking.

Last night, at the folly, things had made sense again. He, Millie. Stability. But once he had gone to bed, it all got jumbled up again. Instead of Millie's warm familiar smile he could only see the wistfulness in Liberty's eyes, relive the moment she had gone on the offensive. Hurting him so that he couldn't hurt her first. Retreating before she was rejected. All she wanted was for someone to put her first. Charlie knew that and yet he had still used her and justified it to himself. Fooled himself.

He could be wrong, of course. Liberty might have meant every bitter word, but he didn't think he was. He knew her, every mercurial shift in mood.

He loved Millie, he always would. But he couldn't ignore that he was *in* love with Liberty any longer. And whatever he did today would hurt one of them, possibly irrevocably.

He leaned on the windowsill, breathing slowly, trying to calm his nerves, wishing Giles would stop hovering ominously and just say whatever was on his mind.

'Charlie... Millie told me, about why the two of you decided to get married so fast.'

There it was. Charlie glanced back at him. 'The way she tells it, that's not the only thing the two of you shared while I was away.'

'I didn't know she... She said that you told her to have a last fling before the ring, if she wanted.'

He attempted a laugh but it fell flat. 'I did, God help me. I thought it would help us both reconcile ourselves to marriage.'

Giles tensed. 'If you're having second thoughts about this wedding, you need to tell Millie.'

Giles was lecturing *him* on *marriage*? On Millie? *Giles* who was too scared to even consider commitment? Who was exactly who Millie didn't need in her life. And yet Charlie had pushed the two of them together and no matter what Millie had said last night she clearly had feelings for his friend.

What kind of marriage would this be when

she had fallen for Giles just as he had fallen for Liberty?

But right now, and more importantly how dare Giles break Millie's heart? 'I'm *not* having second thoughts!' He turned round and faced his best man. 'Millie is one of the best people I know, and I love her. She needs this, and I'd never let her down like that. She wants a family, a happy ever after, and if no one else is going to give it to her,' he added pointedly, 'then I'm damn well going to make sure she gets it, because she deserves *everything*.'

'I know,' Giles said quietly. Too quietly. Charlie stared at his friend and saw the same look he had seen at the rehearsal dinner last night, loss and regret and love.

If so, what was Giles waiting for? 'And what about you, Giles?' he pushed. Now he had started he couldn't stop. His worry about the wedding, his love for Millie, his confusion around Liberty whirling round and round. 'So quick with the advice for others, but what do *you* want? I thought it really was just a fling before the ring between you and Millie, like we agreed. But looking at you now I'm not so sure.'

Giles paled. 'I'll stay away once you're married, Charlie. You know I'd never betray you that way. Millie and I ended everything before we came here. You know I can't give her what she wants.'

Couldn't he? The only thing stopping Giles, that had ever stopped him, were his own doubts and fears. It was so clear—why couldn't Giles see that? 'But you wish you could, don't you?'

His friend turned away, fussing with the tray of buttonholes refusing to answer.

'You're here asking what *I* want, but have you thought about what *you* want?' Charlie was in Giles's space, forcing his friend to concentrate, to listen. 'Or have you spent so long focussing on what you *don't* want—on *not* falling in love, *not* getting married, *not* ending up like your parents, or your sister, or chained to a money pit of a house because of history and society and expectations—that you've forgotten to even *think* about what *you* want?'

For a moment Charlie feared he had gone too far. Giles just stood staring at him, his face so pale it was grey.

But Charlie had to make him see. There was no way he was putting Millie through the humiliation of an abandoned wedding if something, someone better wasn't waiting for her. But how could he marry her knowing she and Giles had feelings for each other?

A saviour complex, Liberty had said. That wasn't always a bad thing and if he could help his two best friends see that they were right for each other then maybe it was actually a very good thing indeed. He was going to tell Liberty that, just as soon as he had sorted these two lovesick fools out. He grinned at Giles, the tension falling away, as the farcical nature of the situation hit him. They just needed French doors and an Edwardian drawing room and they could be characters in a Noel Coward play.

'So. When exactly did you fall in love with my fiancée? And just what are you going to do about it?'

Giles blinked rapidly. 'I need to talk to Millie.'

'I agree, but I think I should speak to her first.' Charlie looked at his watch. The timing couldn't be worse. Guests would be arriving for welcome drinks at any time before heading to the chapel. The last thing any of them needed was his mother or Tabby to suspect anything was wrong before they had sorted it out amongst themselves. 'Go to the chapel as arranged so that Tabby doesn't start panicking. And while you're there, I suggest you start figuring out how you are going to tell my best friend that you love her.'

Charlie wished he felt as confident as he sounded. Breaking off an engagement was tricky at the best of times, even when you were sure the bride didn't want to marry you. Doing it literally minutes before the wedding was filled with pitfalls. What if he didn't find Millie in time and had to add a chapel scene to the play? But luck was with him, he had no sooner headed into the main house than he saw her coming down the stairs, her face lighting up with relief when she saw him. He made his way through the brightly dressed crowd to meet her.

'Want to get out of here for a moment?'

She nodded, and, aware that any moment someone would notice Millie, especially as she was the one in a long white dress, he led the way back upstairs and into a small storage room where they kept his great-grandmother's fur coats.

'You aren't supposed to see me in my wedding dress before the ceremony,' Millie said.

'I think that only counts if the wedding is actually going to take place.' Just saying the words lessened a burden he hadn't realised he was carrying. 'Is it?'

Charlie watched Millie's expression change, from surprise to a slow-dawning relief. 'I… I don't think it can. I'm sorry, Charlie. I can't marry you.'

'Because you're in love with Giles.' He couldn't keep the grin off his face as Millie stared at him wide-eyed.

'You're not…angry?'

How could she think that? He shook his head, injecting as much love and sincerity into his voice as he could. 'I'm not angry. I'm… Honestly, right at this moment, I'm not sure what I am. Except your best friend. I'll always be that.'

'How did we end up here?' Millie asked. "I mean…really?!'

It was amazing to be able to hug her and know they were back to what they had always been, two people who loved and cared about each other deeply. 'I think we both wanted to make each other happy. And maybe we would have done. But it would only ever have been a sort of…' He tried to find the right word.

'Contentment. We'd have been content, I think. Except now we both know there's something more out there, and it's hard to settle for contentment after that.'

'It is.' Charlie kissed the top of her head, before stepping away. 'So I think we'd both better get out there and demand what we *really* want from life. Don't you?'

Charlie did his best to insist that he be the one to go to the chapel and tell the guests that the wedding was off, but Millie was having none of it. 'I'll go,' she said firmly. 'This is a joint decision after all.' Charlie started to argue, but then stopped. It was already mid-afternoon and he had no idea when Liberty was leaving for the airport. He had to get to London as soon as possible to tell her the wedding was off. To tell her he loved her. What happened next was up to her, but he didn't want to leave it a second longer, especially as Tabby was bound to start spreading the news quickly.

'Good luck. With everything,' he said meaningfully, kissing Millie's cheek, then watched her gather up her dress and sprint down the stairs to go and deliver the news and, more importantly, find Giles.

By the time Charlie got downstairs it was empty. If all the guests were at the chapel then Charlie was supposed to be there too, Tabby would be having kittens. Sure enough, when he checked his phone there were several missed calls and texts, the latter all in caps with many exclamation marks. He pocketed his phone and half turned towards the kitchen to get his car keys but stopped as a figure appeared at the front door.

'Am I too late?' Liberty said. 'I want to object.'

Liberty was trembling, but she did her best to hide it. She was about to make herself the most vulnerable she had ever been. Just because she had fallen in love with Charlie didn't mean it was reciprocated. And if it *was* reciprocated that didn't mean he wasn't going to go ahead and get married. This was the man, after all, who allowed the world to think his ex had jilted him to spare her feelings. How likely was he to humiliate his best friend by calling off the wedding?

Talking of whom, why had Millie only just left the house, running down the path, white dress hitched up, too focused to see Liberty? Had she been with Charlie? Surely the groom shouldn't see the bride before the wedding? Whatever they *had* been doing, both were glowing; neither looked like they were exactly being dragged to the altar.

Liberty was suddenly cold. Had she got this very wrong after all? What was she *doing*? The certainty that had propelled her to Euston, over the two hours on the train willing it on and in the taxi from Kings Lynn to Howard Hall began to ebb away.

She finally found her voice. 'What's going on?'

'Millie has gone to tell everyone that the wedding is off.'

'Is it?' She was suddenly light-headed, her voice husky, half formed. 'When did you decide that?'

'About five minutes ago.' Charlie's gaze was direct, but there was a heat in his blue eyes that warmed her through. 'We decided that there was a clear impediment and better to decide now rather than at the altar, even if it's less dramatic.'

She swallowed. 'What was it? The impediment.'

'The small matter that we are both in love with someone else. Turns out Giles was standing in for me in more ways than one. I just wish he had said something earlier but then I can't really talk, can I? Look at how long it took me to figure things out.' He glanced towards the door. 'Soon this place is going to be full of wedding guests enjoying drinks and food even though there was no ceremony, and amongst them will be my mother and sister and I don't know about you but I'm not quite ready to face them. Fancy a walk?'

A *what*? Liberty was still grappling with that casual *in love with someone else*.

Liberty had barely nodded before Charlie took her hand and tugged her through the house to the huge boot room, filled with a collection of old coats, boots, hats, scarves and gloves, grabbing a coat and scarf to put on over his suit, then after checking whether she wanted to borrow anything, out the door and through the gardens. 'At least the path to the beach doesn't take us anywhere near the chapel,' he said.

'Why the beach?' It was like being in some kind of surrealist dream, Alice following the white rabbit. Was she really here or still in bed? Would she wake up and find it was the morning of Christmas Eve and she still had the whole day to endure? But no, she could feel the winter chill on her face, Charlie was beside her, real and solid, his hand holding hers tightly, as if he didn't dare to let her go as he headed to the discreet path which led through the woods towards the sea.

'Because no one will disturb us there.' He checked his watch. 'I can guarantee the house will be filled in less than five minutes and at least half those people will be demanding an explanation from me. That reminds me.' He fished his phone out of his pocket and switched it off without looking at it. 'Let's not make it easy for them. I did wonder about just driving somewhere but I need to face my parents and Tabby at some point. It's not fair to leave this up to Millie and Giles to do alone along with everything else. Besides, there's a twelve-course tasting menu to sample, who wants to miss out on that?'

It sounded rather like he was babbling. Was Charlie *nervous*? The thought gave her strength.

'So, Liberty Gray. I have to ask,' he continued. 'If you hadn't got to the house on time, were you planning to do your objecting in the church?'

'I don't know.' Her stomach swooped at the thought of how very close she had actually come to having to decide. Would she have found the courage to burst in and stop the wedding or would she have bottled it? 'Maybe.'

'I hope you would have waited to the persons here present part,' Charlie said. 'Timing and traditions are so important. But the real question is,' he went on almost conversationally, 'what you wanted to object *to*. Christmas? I know you're not a fan. The very notion of a twelve-course meal? Hereditary titles? I thought,' he added, 'that you were going on holiday.'

He was *definitely* babbling, his conversation jumping all over the place. 'Tomorrow. Thailand.'

'Very nice.' They had finally reached the small, locked gate which led directly from the Howard estate onto the sand dunes. Charlie entered a code and the gate swung open so they could walk through. They were still holding hands, she realised, his fingers firm around hers. He took a deep breath. 'But can any beach beat Norfolk in winter? Just look at those skies.'

Liberty also inhaled, the fresh sea air filling her lungs, and found the courage to say what she had come here to say, with just the gulls and waves as her witness. 'I was going to object to you entering into a marriage with your head not your heart. I was going to tell everyone that I hoped you were in love with me, because I am in love with you. I was going to say that marriage is hard enough without going in with such low expectations and that both you and Millie deserve more.'

They had climbed to the top of the dunes while she was speaking and Charlie halted. The wind was whipping her hair into a tangle, her shoes were covered in sand and her coat inadequate for the wind, but she didn't care, because Charlie's eyes were blazing with love and affection. Love and affection for her. 'That sounds like quite an objection. I think it would have been pretty compelling. It almost makes me wish we'd waited. I almost did,' he said ruefully, cupping her face with his gloved hand. 'I almost left it too late. I knew you were pushing me away, I knew why, but I didn't trust in my own instincts. And I didn't want to let Millie down. Especially not here, in front of my family and friends, knowing how out of place she feels sometimes. But I couldn't ignore the feeling in my gut, the one telling me I was making a colossal mistake. The one telling me that you are worth fighting for and I would be a fool to walk away again. Knowing Giles and Millie have developed feelings for each other made it easier, but I would have called the wedding off this morning regardless. There is only one woman I want to make vows to and she is standing right here.'

'Charlie,' she half whispered.

'I love you, Liberty. I love your courage and kindness. I love your spirit. I love your sense of humour and your intelligence. I love the way you make me feel and the man you make me want to be. I want to date you, properly. To take it slow. To spend time with you with no end date or expectations, but because it's what we both want. I want to hold hands in the street and kiss you on corners, to take you for meals out and spend evenings in, enjoy long lazy days on the beach and long phone calls at night when we're working away. Some of them,' he added, a glint in his eye, 'X-rated. I want all your Christmases and birthdays, to fall more in love with you every day. No more sneaking around, no more pretence. I want honesty.'

Liberty trembled and his hands tightened on hers. 'I know that scares you. Honestly, it scares me too. For me, before, being that vulnerable meant conceding power. Weakness. But love should make us stronger. It took knowing you to realise that.'

'It does scare me,' she admitted. 'But coming

here today scared me and here I am. Because I want all that too. I want it with you. I love you, Charlie Howard, I've loved you for over half my life and if you're with me I'm willing to try.'

He kissed her then, fierce and sweet and she clung to him. 'You're shivering,' he said, taking off his scarf and wrapping it around her neck. 'And I need to go in and face my family. I won't think any less of you if you want to go back to London and avoid all the fallout. You've got a much-deserved holiday to pack for after all.'

'Why don't I postpone the flight for a couple of days? I could always see if I can book another seat, if you wanted to come with me?' she suggested. 'If you don't mind, I think I would like to take Tabby up on her offer of spending Christmas here after all.'

'That sounds like the best Christmas present ever.' He kissed her again. 'Happy Christmas, Liberty. Let this be the first of many.'

'I like the idea of that.' And as they walked back towards the estate, Liberty realised that she was looking forward to Christmas for the first time she could remember, because she had everything she wanted, right here.

EPILOGUE

One year later

'CHARLIE, YOU LOOK so handsome.'

Charlie turned and looked at his sister. 'What's happened? Is Liberty okay?'

Tabby shook her head. 'Honestly, that's your first thought? Not "Thank you, Tabby, you look beautiful too"?'

'You do look beautiful,' he said quickly. She did, of course, in her long silk dress of dull gold teamed with a cream faux fur cape, her hair piled up on top of her head, small gold stars holding it in place.

'That's better. Liberty is having some photos taken so I thought I would check in on you. Make sure you are okay—that you are still planning on turning up for *this* wedding.'

'Very funny.' He felt suddenly cold. 'Liberty isn't having second thoughts, is she?'

'No, panic not. Where are Millie and Giles? Shouldn't they be looking after you?'

'Millie is resting before the ceremony and you know what Giles is like. He doesn't like her to be alone for too long.'

'The devoted father-to-be, who would have thought it? And who would have thought that my big brother would be marrying my best friend? I hope you know I will always take her side in arguments.'

'I wouldn't expect anything less.' Charlie smiled at his sister. 'Thank you. Organising one wedding for me was one thing but to organise a second just one year later...'

'And with even less notice,' Tabby said meaningfully. 'I actually did this for Liberty. I didn't see why she should suffer for your sins. Besides, it's so small, and everything is in place at Glenmere so there was hardly anything to do.'

This time Charlie had been involved every step of the way, making sure the wedding was exactly what Liberty wanted. They were holding it at Glenmere of course, the place where it had all begun, a pared-down guest list, just a handful of friends each, his immediate family, and, those of hers who had accepted. In the end she had invited them all, and to her amazement most had accepted even without the inducement of magazine coverage. Both Giles and Millie were acting as best man, Tabby as maid of honour, the bridesmaids Liberty's youngest siblings.

No twelve-course tasting menu, no ostentation, just as simple as a wedding in a castle could be. It was small, quiet and utterly perfect.

'No nerves?' Tabby asked.

'Only that she'll change her mind. I think a third failed engagement would be more than I can live down.'

His sister grinned. 'Third time lucky. Don't worry, Charlie. This time you've managed to propose to the right bride. She'll be there.'

The chapel at Glenmere had been transformed thanks to Millie's clever work, cream and gold garlands brightening the rather austere grey walls and simple pews, the same colours repeated in the large floral arrangements on the altar and at every corner of the chapel. Liberty smoothed down her cream silk skirt and adjusted her veil. She wasn't nervous, to her surprise, just eager to be married.

The guests were all seated, waiting, apart from Giles and Millie who stood with Charlie by the altar. Charlie was nervous, she could tell by the way he fidgeted, the quirk in his mouth, how pale he was. On one side were his family and friends, on the other hers, and she still couldn't believe how many had made the effort to be here on New Year's Eve, even Orlando flying in from LA for the occasion. She would never have a normal family, but Charlie had helped her accept the one she had, given her the courage to reach out to them. Which was why her father stood by her side and her father's twins and her sisters on her mother's side were clustered around Tabitha, in cream dresses with gold sashes. She had let Felix off the role of pageboy, he had looked so appalled at the suggestion.

'Ready?' her father asked and she nodded.

'Absolutely.'

She'd been ready since Charlie Howard had smiled at her the first time she had visited his house, since all those times when he had been kind to his sister's lonely friend, since that first kiss.

He had kept his word and wooed her patiently and slowly for most of the last year until Liberty had decided enough was enough, taken him to Paris and proposed to him. She would have been happy with an elopement, but they had already decided on a family Christmas and New Year's at Glenmere. Combining the festive season with their wedding made sense. Only not Christmas, she had said, especially as that was the anniversary of his last wedding. New Year's Eve was where it had begun for them. It was the perfect day to start their next step.

The music started and her sisters started their

solemn march down the short aisle, the twins holding their posies tightly, then Tabby sauntered down as if it was a catwalk, winking at Orlando as she went. And then it was time. The small congregation were on their feet, everyone turning to watch her, phones out and recording, but all she could see was Charlie, smiling at her, his face alive with love.

'Hi,' Charlie whispered. 'You look beautiful.'

She grinned back, taking his outstretched hand. 'You showed up.'

'Always and forever,' he promised.

As they turned to face the vicar, she knew that he had made the most important vow already. There were no guarantees in life but with Charlie by her side she could face anything and she couldn't wait to get started.

* * * * *

If you missed the previous story in the Blame It on the Mistletoe duet, then check out

Christmas Bride's Stand-In Groom
by Sophie Pembroke

And if you enjoyed this story, check out these other great reads from Jessica Gilmore

It Started with a Vegas Wedding
Christmas with His Ballerina
The Princess and the Single Dad

All available now!

HARLEQUIN
Reader Service

Enjoyed your book?

Try the perfect subscription for Romance readers and get more great books like this delivered right to your door.

See why over 10+ million readers have tried Harlequin Reader Service.

Start with a Free Welcome Collection with free books and a gift—valued over $20.

Choose any series in print or ebook.
See website for details and order today:

TryReaderService.com/subscriptions